Mountain Storms

"Wild Freedom" first appeared as a six-part serial under the
George Owen Baxter byline in Street & Smith's *Western Story
Magazine* (11/11/22–12/16/22). Copyright © 1922 by Street &
Smith Publications, Inc. Copyright © renewed 1950 by
Dorothy Faust. Copyright © 2004 by Golden West Literary
Agency for restored material. Acknowledgment is made to
Condé Nast Publications, Inc., for their co-operation.

First Edition
First Printing: August 2004

Published in 2004 in conjunction with
Golden West Literary Agency.

Set in 11 pt. Plantin by Al Chase.

Printed in the United States on permanent paper.

Library of Congress Cataloging-in-Publication Data

Brand, Max, 1892–1944.
    Mountain storms : a western story / by Max Brand.—1st ed.
      p. cm.
    ISBN 1-59414-001-4 (hc : alk. paper)
    1. Western stories.   I. Title.
PS3511.A87M64 2004
   813´.54—dc22   2004047080

Mountain Storms

A Western Story

MAX BRAND®

Five Star • Waterville, Maine

Mountain Storms

Chapter One

WHERE DANGER STALKS

No seasoned mountaineer would have tried to cross the mountain range encumbered as John Parks was, and with the cloud streamers blown out stiffly from the summits and snapping off little fleecy bits that the wind hurried across the sky. Even in the lowlands the norther had spread an Arctic chill, and the bald heights must be insufferably cold. To be sure, the trip would have been practicable enough to warmly dressed, active men, but the little burro would slow the pace of the journey to a dreary crawl, and, besides, there was Tommy to think of. Hardened far beyond city children by this three years in the mountains, still, at twelve, there is a marked limit to a boy's endurance. He was already fagged by the journey, for, although they had come only ten miles since morning, it had been bitter work for Tommy up and down the hills, and it might be ten miles more across the summits and down to shelter on the farther side.

John Parks consulted his son.

"We could camp over yonder, Tommy," he said. "You see that little hollow with the pines standing around it?"

Tommy looked, and his heart went out to the circle among the trees as though the night had already closed and the evergreens were full of shine and shadow from a fire built in their midst.

"But," went on John Parks, "it's not far past noon, and

just over that next crest is the place."

He lifted his gaunt face with that strange smile that Tommy knew so well. All his life he had seen his father looking far off from the sorrows of every day to a bright to-morrow.

"So what do you think, Tommy?" John Parks asked, resting his hand on the shoulder of his son. "Do you think we could make it without tiring you out?"

The wind stooped against them and passed an icy thrill through the body of the boy, but, when he looked up, he found the smile still on his father's face as though he heard already the far-off murmur of the Turnbull River. What a weary way they had come to find that promised land.

"Oh," he said, "I can make it, Dad. You don't need to worry about me."

The hand closed on his shoulder.

"Ah, you're a tough fellow, Tommy," said John Parks. "We'll try it, then."

They trudged on, the burro grunting and switching his tail before them. They climbed 2,000 feet in three miles with the trees dwindling and dwarfing until they came to a waist-high hedge of lodgepole pine, willow, and tough shrubs at timber-line, a hedge shaved level across the top by the edge of storm winds, running in and out along the mountainsides at one height like the verge of green water. Above was the bald region of the summit. The sun had melted the surface snow; the wind had frozen it again, and now it blazed like glass. That was poor footing for the climb. Even the burro, as it pressed out from the thicket, shrank with a tentative hoof. Moreover, the wind now leaped into their faces. It flattened the burro's ears and drove his tail straight out. Tommy looked up in dismay, but John Parks shook a bony hand above his head.

"They can't beat us, Tommy!" he shouted. "It takes more than wind and weather to beat us!"

"No, Dad, we'll make it," Tommy tried to say, but the wind passed his lips and blew a stiff pocket in one cheek, so he put down his head and staggered on in the lee of John Parks. Then his father took his hand, and with that aid he managed to keep steadily at work. When John Parks looked down at him, he even managed a pinch-faced smile, but all the time the core of warmth at his heart was shrinking, and the numbing cold spread swiftly up to his shoulders, then up his legs to the knees, to the hips. He centered all his mind, all his will, on every step he made, but, oh, the weariness that the cold was bringing home to him!

A fresher blast caught him and wrenched him to the side against John Parks.

"Steady, Tommy!" cried his father. "It's all downhill now. Don't you see? We're going to make it easily, boy!"

It was true, for, when Tommy looked ahead, there was no longer that soul-taking, upward slope. Instead, his eye pitched down past the snow fields to the dark streak of timberline, and past timberline to a great, green valley with a river running straight as a silver arrow through its heart. That was the promised land, then, and yonder was the Turnbull. Here was the place where his father's traps every day would take full toll, where the deer came up to the edge of the campfire to watch and wonder, where the cabin was to rise, where the ground would be cleared.

He pushed himself away from John Parks and with a cry made the first step down the slope. His legs buckled. Their strength around the knees had turned to water, and he pitched down on his face. His heart swelled with grief. Now, indeed, he had shamed himself. All the praise for strength and for stolid endurance that had been showered on him during the journey was thrown away through this hideous weakness. He strove to raise himself, but his elbows were like his knees, unstrung and helpless.

John Parks scooped the small body up and stood with it crushed to him. Poor Tommy looked up into a face that was wild with terror.

"I'm only winded!" he cried faintly. "And I slipped. I can go on now, Dad."

But, while one arm drew him closer to a bony breast, the other was thrown to the sky.

"Heaven forgive me. Heaven help me," murmured John Parks.

He lowered Tommy gently to the snow, and there he lay limply. Even the hot shame could not nerve him as he watched his father strip off his coat. Tommy was raised and wrapped in the garment closely while John Parks cried: "Oh, Tommy, hold on . . . fight hard. I'll be down to the trees in no time. Fight, Tommy!"

The burro was left to follow aimlessly in the rear, shaking his head at the wind, while John Parks stumbled and slipped and ran down the slope. Tommy tried to protest. He knew well enough that it was dangerous for a man to run unprotected into the face of that icy wind, but, when he tried to speak, his voice became an unintelligible gibbering. Presently his mind became as numb as his body. Thought formed dimly as dream figures. Sometimes it seemed to him that the wind had lifted them and was sweeping them back to the terrible summit. Then the gasping voice of John Parks would come to him like a hand pushing away clouds of sleep: "Fight, Tommy. Oh, Tommy, keep fighting!" Yet the drowsiness increased. He began to wonder why they did not stop, now that they had found such a pleasant time for sleeping.

At length his father was no longer slipping as he ran. The

strong, sweet breath of evergreens was filling his nostrils, and suddenly he was dropped to the ground. The shock recalled him enough to clear his eyes, but it was not until John Parks had torn dead branches from the trees, had piled them, had kindled them to a flame, that he understood. The first yellow leap of the fire told him how near he had been to death, and now he was placed on the very verge of the fire while his father, gasping and coughing, pummeled his body and rubbed the blood into circulation. In half an hour he was tingling painfully in hands and feet. His face was swollen with heat. But the danger was gone, and, as if to prove that all was well again, the burro stumbled into the clearing and stood with one long ear tilted forward to the fire.

Chapter Two

ALONE WITH BILLY

There followed a drowsy time for Tommy. Now and again he was roused with a sudden shuddering to a memory of the labor up the mountainside. But those daylight touches of realization were only momentary. On the whole, he was lost in warm content by the fire. He roused himself for five minutes to drink coffee and eat bacon and flapjacks. But after that he sank back into a semi-trance. Afterward, he could remember seeing and wondering at the livid face of his father and the great, feverish, bright eyes of John Parks as he fell asleep.

In that sleep he was followed by dreams of disaster. He found himself again struggling up an endless slope of ice-glazed snow, with the wind shrieking into his face and tugging at his body, while his father strode before him with long steps, tossing up his arms to the driving clouds and laughing like a maniac.

Once he came dimly half awake and actually heard the voice of John Parks, laughing and crying out near him. It seemed odd to him that his father should be talking like this in the middle of the night, but sleep had half numbed his brain, and he was unconscious again in a moment.

He only wakened with the sun fully in his face and shoved himself up on his arms and blinked about him. The nightmare gradually lifted from his brain. He was able to see that the little clearing in which the fire had been made the night

12

before, the embers of which were still sending up a tiny drift of smoke, was fringed with young aspens, now newly leafed with sprays of young yellow-green—almost more yellow than green as the sun shone through the fresh-sprouting foliage. And yonder was the burro, absurdly nibbling at the sprouts on a bush and paying no heed to the rich grass.

"Oh, Dad!" called Tommy, rubbing the sleep out of his eyes.

There was no answer. The silence swept suddenly around him and became an awful thing. At a little distance, a confused roaring and dashing that had troubled his sleep he now made out to be the voice of a river. They must be close, then, to the bank of the river; it was that famous Turnbull River of which they had heard so much. As for the absence of his father, that could be explained by the fact that he had gone fishing to take their breakfast out of the water.

So Tommy stood up and stretched himself carefully. To his surprise, there was nothing wrong with him, more than a drowsiness and lethargy of the muscles, if it might be called that. Before he had taken half a dozen steps about the clearing, that lethargy was departing. The very first glance told him that surmise had been correct. A trail well defined in the rain-softened ground led away from the camp in the direction of the river.

He followed the trail easily, but as he went, his wonder grew, for the signs wandered back and forth drunkenly. Sometimes the steps were short, sometimes they were long. Here he had stumbled and lurched sidewise against a young sapling, as the damaged branches showed as did a deep footprint at its base as well. Tommy paused and drew a breath of dismay. Something was decidedly wrong. His father was no expert mountaineer, he knew. When the doctor's orders, three years before, had sent poor John Parks in search of health in the open country, he had been a great deal of a tenderfoot. And at his age it was impossible to learn all that he needed to know about mountain life and mountain ways. But to have made this trail required that a man should have walked in the darkness, stumbling here and there. If John Parks had walked away from the camp in the darkness. . . .

Here the mind of Tommy trembled and drew back from the conclusion that had jumped upon him full-grown. Before his mother's death, he had heard her once in a raving delirium. Now, as he thought back to the husky, harsh voice of his father nearby him in the darkness, he felt certain that John Parks, also, must have been delirious. Yes, that was it, for, otherwise, men did not waken and laugh so wildly in the heart of the night. Why had he not wakened the instant he heard that laughter and taken care of the older man?

Tommy hurried on along the trail. It was more and more sadly evident that something had gone wrong as the trail reeled onward. It reached a grove of close-standing, lodgepole pines. Apparently John Parks had been unable to find his way among them. Here and again he had attempted to go through and had recoiled after running into a trunk. Finally he had given up the effort, and the trail wound fifty feet to the left.

By this time Tommy was half blind with fear and bewilderment, and he ran on, panting, his feet slipping on the wet grass. Momently the noise of the Turnbull grew louder, and at length he came through a scattered screen of trees with the dash of a waterfall making the ground beneath his feet tremble. A hundred feet above him, the smooth, green water slid over the edge of a cliff, surrounded itself with a lace of white spray as it fell, and then the solid column was powdered on the rocks, spread out again in a black, swirling pool, and finally emptied into a long, flume-like channel down which the current raced like galloping horses.

Where the bank rose sheerly, twenty feet above the edge of that whirling pool, the tracks of his father ceased. Tommy, strangled with fear, looked up to the pale blue sky above him. By an effort into which all his will was thrown, he managed to look down again—then fell on his knees, moaning.

To his eyes the whole matter was as clear as though he had read it in the pages of a book. Here the ground on the lip of the bank had been gouged away by the feet of John Parks as the poor man slipped and fell. Whirling in that fall, he had reached out with both hands. There one had slipped on the wet grass. There the other of them had caught at a small shrub and torn it out by the roots. Finally there was the place where both hands had taken their last hold on the edge of the bank—a hold beneath which the dirt had melted away and had let him drop straight to water below.

Tommy cleared his dizzy eyes and crept closer. There was no hope that John Parks could have lived for a moment in that run of waters. A twig was dislodged by Tommy's hand and fell into the stream. It was whirled wildly around, danced away from the teeth of jag-toothed rocks, and then darted off down the foaming length of the flume. A tree trunk might be ground to powder in that shoot of water.

Tommy drew back from the water. The moment the bank cut away the view of the stream, he turned and fled as though the waterfall were a living enemy ready to plunge in pursuit with mighty leaps. Breathless, he reached the clearing. He ran to the burro, he threw his arms around the neck of that scrawny little beast.

"Oh, Billy," he cried, "Dad is gone . . . Dad is gone! Dad can never come back to me!"

Billy canted one ear back and one forward, as was his way in all emergencies calling for thought, and, swinging his head around, he looked mildly upon his young master. The next instant he was calmly reaching for more buds on the shrub off which he had been feeding.

Tommy stepped back and watched the burro calmly making a meal, stamping now and then to show his content, or flicking his long ears back in gloomy anger when he caught sight of the pack saddle nearby. It seemed to Tommy Parks that the patient munching of the burro was a symbol of the bland indifference of all the world. His father was dead, but here was the wind bustling merrily among the twinkling leaves of the aspens, and yonder were the white heights over which they had just come, and in the distance was the voice of the Turnbull, an ominous, small thunder. His father was dead, but all went on as it had gone on before. The very fire that he had lighted still sent up a straggling wisp of smoke. At sight of this, Tommy, who had remained dry-eyed, suddenly burst into tears and wept in an agony of grief and loneliness and fear.

The burro wandered over and curiously nudged his shoulder with his nose.

Chapter Three

THE MARAUDER KILLS

When a man is lost in the woods, the first thing to do is to sit down and have a long think and not wander away in the first direction that comes into his head. That was what John Parks had cautioned Tommy more than once. He remembered it now as he sat cross-legged under a pine, with his head back against the trunk. He had spent the morning making up the pack—a weird bundle it was when he finished—and moving down lower in the valley, farther from the Turnbull, so that the sound of its roaring would not haunt him. He had descended simply because he dared not undertake, alone, that perilous journey over the mountain snows. No, wherever he went, it must be down the valley.

He made the first stop at this open place where the lower slope of the mountain put out a fist through the shrouding forest—or, rather, it might be called a sharp, square shoulder. From the top of it Tommy looked up and down the valley across a wilderness of evergreens. The great mountains over which they had come were at his back. Beneath him, the Turnbull wound into view again, making him shudder as the sun flashed on its windings. In the slim distance were other mountains, a cloudy rolling of blue that separated to give place to the Turnbull.

Through that pass he must go with Billy. It might take weeks to reach the gap, and during that time he might find no

17

man to help him on the way. Yes, and what lay in blue distance and under the horizon, he could not dream. Perhaps there was a desert, burning hot, impassable except to those who knew the water holes, deadly even to those, sometimes. He had heard much of such places.

As for the trail over which he had come, if he turned back, he would have first the terrible heights of the mountains to climb, and then, beyond those, there would be the long stretches that he had crossed with his father—and it had taken them three days from the nearest town. He might miss the way altogether, besides. And it would not be strange if one perished of hunger. No, the best way, he decided, was to follow the Turnbull River, even though it wandered down through an eternity of distance. For there was a great chance that it would lead him to some town.

Bravely, but not quickly, he made up his mind. That uncertain distance was terrible to poor Tommy. For hours he sat there pondering the question back and forth, and, when he eventually made up his mind and rose to start on with Billy, he suddenly noted that his feet were in shadow. The afternoon had worn late, all unawares.

He wanted to start at once, for he was in a fever of eagerness to have the first stage of the great adventure accomplished and put behind him, but he knew that, when one finds a good camping place in the middle of the afternoon, it is better to camp at once and make an early start in the morning. Nothing could be more ideal than this level hill shoulder.

In the dense ranks of the trees that marched up around him, there were quantities of dead branches. His keen young eye had noted them automatically while he sat there during the afternoon. There were shrubs, too, which he could easily cut with the sharp axe of his father. Wood, then, which is one of the two main essentials for a camp, was there in plenty. As for water, it was furnished in equal abundance. A rivulet flowed from the mouth of a cave that had doubtless been worn by the working of the water, and the little stream wound across the level, then darted with sudden speed to the foot of the hill where it joined a large creek, and both went murmuring off to join the more distant Turnbull. Perhaps John Parks, if he had seen this place, would have decided to start his home on the very spot. With that thought, great tears welled into the eyes of Tommy.

But, according to John Parks, there is a great and universal antidote for sorrow—work. Tommy sprang up and set to making camp with a fury. He took the pack from the back of Billy—his unpracticed hands had built it so poorly that it had twisted awry on the burro's patient back—and then, with Billy at work on the grass, the boy hurried to the trees and swung the axe with a will.

It was far too large for him, but practice had taught him to shorten his grip on the handle, and in that fashion he made fair play with it. Its keen edge gave him in five minutes an abundance of wood that kept him busy for half an hour longer, dragging it to the center of the opening. But he wanted an oversupply of fuel; there could not be too much to furnish him with company during the cold, solemn hours of the night.

The fire itself he made in approved fashion, grouping some big stones around it, and here he mixed the cornmeal with soda and water and salt, and fried his hot cakes and set his bacon sizzling. He made coffee, too, and for a while he was so busy that he had no time to give to other worries.

It was not until he began to eat his supper that grief took him by the throat. It seemed to Tommy that John Parks was somewhere down the mountain, was coming home with great, impatient strides, and that his well-known whistle would surely soon be sounding on the farther side of the clearing. Once he found himself breathlessly listening, his eyes strained and wide. He rallied from that with a great effort, but, when his glance lowered, it struck on the side of the coffee pot, with the graniteware dented where he, on a morning, had dropped pot and coffee and all and sent the boiling stuff sizzling across his father's shoes. He chuckled softly as he remembered how John Parks had danced around on one foot, and then on the other. But there had been no reproving, no sharp words.

Tommy buried his face in his hands and sat quivering, full of a grief that could not spend itself in tears. Afterward, he could eat no more. He could not even look at the tinware and the pots, but, turning his back on the camp, he fled uphill and down, fairly running from sorrow. In a measure, he succeeded, for he came to a panting halt at last with the thick forest around him, rapidly darkening with evening, and realized that he must work back carefully if he expected to find the camp.

So that problem filled his mind, and, when he reached the camp, it was to find the fire almost dead. He freshened it, and, as he did so, he heard, blown on the wind from lower down in the valley, a shrill, quavering, sobbing voice, melancholy as the weeping of a lost child. Tommy listened with a chill running up his spine, for well he knew it was a mountain lion hunting up the valley, hunting for the time being, carelessly and well-nigh blindly, since he chose to come down the wind instead of against it. And hungered pumas have been known to stalk men, if not actually attack them.

Tommy, at least, could collect half a hundred memories of stories such as men tell around a campfire when supper is finished and the day's work is done and pipes and imaginations are drawing freely. He picked up the rifle, saw that it was loaded, and practiced aiming it here and there wherever the firelight flashed on a leaf. It was a heavy gun for a child to handle, but familiarity with one's tools is half the battle, and for two years now John Parks had taken an almost foolish pleasure in teaching his son to shoot with that very weapon.

When Tommy started to work cleaning up the supper dishes, he kept the rifle close at hand. Then he built a rousing fire, not of loose brush that would toss flames into the sky for a few wild minutes and then burn out, but of solid branches that would keep a blaze alive for hours. He even ventured into the forest for more wood, but it was only a single expedition, for, while he worked, he felt eyes watching him in the darkness.

But when he went back to the fire and lay down beside it, twisted in his blanket, only one side was sheltered by the heat of the fire and the red light that all wild beasts are said to dread. The other side lay open to the terrible dark and all the powers that prey by night.

There had been no such fear, no dream of such fear the other nights when John Parks was near. The very sound of his voice, so it seemed to the boy, would be sufficient to frighten hungered prowlers away. Night had been simple and even beautiful before. But now, as he looked up to the huge arch of the sky, filled with impersonal eyes, the mountains appearing like piled shadows on the one side, it seemed to Tommy that all the vast space in between was packed close with enmity and hatred focusing on his single head.

He got up again, dry of throat, and with his eyes burning from constant staring among the trees and the shadows. This time he split the fire into two parts, each a solid mass of wood that should burn steadily without replenishing until close to daylight, and between the two fires he lay down.

It was very hot there. He folded the blanket and lay on top of it. He even opened his shirt so that the air might cool him. But it was better a thousand times to lie in heat than in terror.

That one cry from the mountain lion was all he heard, however; perhaps it had been hurrying across country on a trail well known to it and leading to certain prey. That was the reason it had been traveling down the wind, instead of prowling up it.

This conclusion came like a blessing and the assurance of peace to Tommy. An instant later the stars swam and mingled together in a soft, cool fire above his head. He slept.

It was no nightmare now. Utter weariness of soul and body shut out the possibility of dreams. Out of that dreamless, perfect sleep he was wakened by the horrible knife-stab of sound—the snarl of a wild beast making a kill and biting deeply. He stood erect, his heart thundering wildly, his wits astray. Then he heard a groan and a fall.

For the first time he could see. The two fires on which he had counted so certainly had burned to smoldering beds of coals, dusted over with ashes that alone kept the life from completely dying. From the beds of coals there passed an uncertain glow of light that revealed things not at a glance but by dim degrees, just as the mind works out a problem.

So, what Tommy saw first was a distant, isolated gleam on a polished leaf. Next he saw the pack, a jumbled heap without head or tail to it. Last of all he saw where Billy lay prostrate, and over the poor burro, with fangs sunk in his throat, crouched the mountain lion, a tawny splotch in the darkness—although clearly enough visible for Tommy to make out the long sweep of the tail as it was lashed from side to side.

He cried out in an agony of horror and fear, but the small, choked voice had the power to make the puma leap, growling, from its kill and face suddenly around. There it saw a man from the ground, risen out of the very body of detested fires, so it seemed. The mountain lion spat in fear and rage, then turned and with uncanny speed slunk away. A single stride, and it seemed to melt into nothingness.

But Tommy dared not move. It was not fear of the lion that kept him frozen and still. A danger once confronted and seen nakedly with the eye becomes only a tithe as terrible as when it existed only behind a wall of darkness. It was not dread of the lion, but consciousness of what the death of Billy meant—that he was chained to this place in the valley of the Turnbull River. He could not venture farther away than a single day's march from his source of supplies, and, in this wilderness, how long would it be before men came that way?

Chapter Four

TOOLS FOR THE BATTLE

Large meanings sometimes burst upon the brain with one flash that shows all the corners of their significance. So it was with Tommy. In the horror of that great knowledge, he forgot fear of the monster that had only now crouched in the clearing scarcely more than leaping distance away from him. He forgot the death of the poor burro, although the old ways and the patient soul of Billy had made him an old and dear friend. Only one soul-crushing thought remained—that he was marooned here in the wilderness as completely as though he were his favorite Robinson Crusoe on the island. Rifle, ammunition, the bundle of traps, clothing, food—all of these were things that he needed to sustain life, and he could not take them with him a single step now that Billy was dead.

But was Billy, indeed, dead? In an agony of haste, forgetful entirely of all danger of the mountain lion that might still be lurking near the edge of the clearing, he raced to Billy and dropped to his knees. But Billy was dead. His lolling tongue, his torn throat, told plainly that he would never rise again. Tommy sank back on the ground. He looked up and saw the cold beginnings of the dawn make the stars fade slowly. Still his brain struggled with the future. He was only twelve. If he had a rest for a rifle, he could shoot and shoot well; his three years among the mountains had taught him much about them. But, after the ammunition was gone, how could he

24

live? And in this wilderness, would the lonely life be endurable?

No tears came. He had been snatched into the heart of a tragedy so swiftly that he could not weep. After all, tears came more quickly when there is a comforter nearby. There in the cold grass he lay, his fists clenched tightly, struggling against the problem. It would be easier and less painful to go back to that fatal place on the brink of the river and cast himself in. But now the light of morning increased rapidly, and to the east he saw the first sunlight glisten on the top of a snowy mountain.

Tommy rose slowly to his feet, and he was no sooner risen than he was touched by that spur which drives men on to most of their accomplishments—a stab of hunger. An instant later, he was busy kindling the fire. He had begun to slice bacon, but a moment of reflection made him drop the knife. This was food that would keep, and there might well come a time when he would need it bitterly. In the meantime, that spring morning held other life that must feed him. A tree squirrel chattered overhead and told him that he need not hunt far. So he took up the ever-loaded rifle, dropped upon one knee, with his elbow resting on the other, and took careful aim. The squirrel promptly ducked around to the farther side of the tree trunk. But Tommy knew squirrel nature. The little creatures are invincibly curious, and, instead of moving around to the farther side of the tree to get in a shot, he watched the same opening among the branches. Presently, as he had expected, the tiny head slipped into view, and that instant his finger closed on the trigger.

He did not miss. When one has a limited supply of ammunition, one dare not miss. The ring of the shot was still in his ears when he heard the little body come rustling through the foliage and drop with a light thud to the ground. He took it up quickly with a strangely savage thrill of satisfaction. Was not all the world now banded against him? John Parks had stood between him and the outside, but now he was stripped naked of help. Every tooth and claw hidden among those tree-clad valleys and lowlands were against him. And he had struck his first blow in self-defense.

The squirrel he cleaned and broiled for his breakfast. It was a big, fat fellow and made enough of a meal, even eaten without bread—for the cornmeal was something that he must scrupulously cherish against a time of need. When the meal was ended, his spirits had risen greatly. John Parks, after breakfast, had always sat quietly and smoked a pipe while he arranged all his plans for the day's work. Tommy imitated that good example by sitting up, hugging his knees while he surveyed the situation.

There was one advantage, at least. So long as misfortune had to overtake him, it was the greatest blessing that he had been struck here, where the cumbrous pack was left in such an ideal camping place. Water, wood, and, best of all, for a year-around home, a permanent shelter made to his hand, for such the cave, from which the little stream ran, seemed to offer. He went instantly to explore it.

It was far better than he had dared to hope. It opened as a roughly rectangular gap six or seven feet across and about half that height. But almost immediately it expanded to better proportions. It swelled up a dozen feet high and twice that broad, and in the dim light Tommy could see the glimmer of the stream trailing off into indistinguishable darkness.

He went back to the embers of his breakfast fire, picked out a length of resinous pinewood for a torch, lighted it, and with that yellow sputter of flame he advanced again in the cave. Now he could make out every detail. It drove back into the heart of the mountain nearly a hundred feet, with an arched roof of rock and rough rock walls that seemed to promise that there could never be a cave-in. Toward the rear, the dimensions of the cave steadily shrank until it ended in a little crevice of a hand's breadth, out of which the water poured.

What could have been more perfect as a natural home? The heart of Tommy swelled with the delight of a conqueror. He began to feel that, after all, his might not be a losing fight. There would be ways of making the struggle, and, although it might be bitter, was it not possible that he might stay on there until other men came that way? And surely they must come sooner or later, and, when they arrived in the valley, they must find signs that would lead them to his cave.

That thought inspired him to a new labor. But first of all he moved some burning embers of the fire to the front of the cave, and a little to the side. That must be his permanent fireplace, and he must never let the fire die lest his supply of matches should be exhausted. That could be arranged by a skillful laying of the fire.

Next he brought in all the pack, bit by bit, and distributed the articles on natural shelves of the rock where moisture would not get at them. When all was stowed away, it was a small beginning, indeed, and few tools for a twelve-year-old to use in his battle for life.

There was the body of poor Billy to be disposed of before it should become a problem. He decided that he would dig a hole just beside the body, so that Billy would slide into it. Then the dead burro could be covered over and the burial properly completed. That work could be done with the shovel that had always been a part of John Parks's pack. But this could be left until the morrow. Other pressing things remained to be accomplished at once.

First of all, he must not venture out without a weapon. So he tried his father's big Colt, in its holster, at his hip—it extended clear to his knee—and took the axe. He set out for the river, since it seemed to him that travelers would be most apt to come up or down its course, and, as he went, he left a blazed trail on the trees, making the marks so closely together that they would be sure to catch the eye in a continuous line.

A full four miles he continued until, leg weary from the walk and arm weary from wielding the heavy axe, he came to the edge of the stream. Its course was no longer fenced with steep cliffs here, but the water spread out over a wide, shallow channel, with broad-topped rocks gleaming just beneath the surface. By the shore he marked half a dozen pools where there must surely be excellent fishing. Here he blazed the trees, hewing off big sections of the bark and the surface wood to catch the eye of any wayfarer.

After that he rested an hour and started back along his own blazed trail. A mile from camp he stumbled across a big mountain grouse. He knocked the bird over with a luckily aimed rock and then wrung its neck, and, as he marched on again with his dinner in his hand, he found himself whistling. He stopped short to wonder at himself.

After all, he told himself, it had not been an unhappy morning. That blazed trail was certain to take the eye of some wandering trapper who would follow the sign to Tommy's camp, and the stranger would lead him back into the world. The newborn hope straightway became a surety. It was a matter of only a few days, a few weeks at the most, before he would be discovered. Surely he could contain himself that long!

Coming onto the clearing again, he was shocked by the sight of the open entrance to the cave. He hurried in, but all was as he had left it. No prowling beast had taken advantage of his negligence to rob him of his store of food. He broiled the grouse and ate, and afterward he set about blocking the entrance to the cave.

It was not hard to do. There was a profusion of big rocks around the opening, and these he rolled into the entrance, walling it up solidly. Half a dozen stones in the center were of a size that he could easily handle, and these could be moved and removed when he returned to camp at the end of a day's hunting, or left it in the morning.

By the time this was accomplished, he was tired, but here remained many a stretch of territory that must be explored. So he sallied out with axe and revolver once more and took the opposite direction, going up the slope toward the higher mountain.

There was far less likelihood of men straying through this region, and therefore he made his blazes fewer and farther between. In time he came out on an open place littered with the rocks of a recent small landslide that had scraped down the hillside beyond and sent a wash of boulders and small rocks across this comparative level. The sight caused Tommy to pause with concern, and he looked back down the slope in the direction of his camp. Suppose such a slide as this one should start and continue with greater volume down the hill—might he not be buried in his cave?

But he remembered a favorite saying of John Parks: "A man has to take chances of one kind or another." And he turned to continue on his way. As he did so, however, his eye caught a motion among the rocks. He stopped short again, thrilling with fear. Just what had moved, he could not tell. He had a general impression, a chance-caught glimpse, rather than a definite picture. He jerked out the revolver. It was far too heavy for him, so he dropped down on one knee and supported the gun on the other. When in danger of wild beasts, he had learned long before, one must stand one's ground, no matter with what fear. Man has no speed of foot, no escape, and flight simply invites pursuit.

But his heart was hammering at the base of his throat, filling his whole body with trembling, when he saw it again—a bit of fur stirring behind a rock—the gleam of bright eyes. Suddenly the whole head of a little bear cub no bigger than a rabbit popped into view, surveyed him intently for an instant, and disappeared again.

There is nothing more intriguing than a newborn cub, but Tommy felt no pleasure. A youngster of that age must be close to its mother, and mother grizzlies are apt to be incarnate fiends if they think that their offspring are in danger. Where was she now? He recalled a score of stories about the almost human intelligence of grizzlies, how they hide their trails when they are hunted, how they have been known to double back, more than once, and hunt the hunter.

Perhaps this old vixen was engaged in that occupation even now. Perhaps she was shielding herself behind one of the boulders just to his rear, creeping up silently—very silently— in spite of all her bulk. It seemed to Tommy that the air was suddenly rank with the odor of bear. He jerked his head around with a low gasp and stared behind him. He could see nothing, but at the same time, as though she had seen his fear and decided to lurk no longer, the great battle roar of a grizzly flooded around him, deafened him, seemed to pour out of the very ground on which he stood.

He leaped to his feet. He would have fled, if he could, but now he could not stir a muscle. Still that shambling, monstrous form that he expected did not come. The hollow echoes of the roar died off down the hillside, shattering to silence among the more distant trees. What did it mean? He could not flee, because he might run into the jaws of the great brute or within striking distance of a paw whose lightest stroke might smash his skull or crush his body.

Again the roar burst out at him, but this time, plainly, it was on the farther side of the rock jumble, pouring out of the earth. A furious scratching began at the same time, and a great boulder that leaned against the slope quivered out— then fell back with a jar. At the same instant, two little grizzly cubs jumped into view among the rocks and scurried as fast as their short legs would carry them for the great stone that had just been moved. Around the corner of it they darted and disappeared. The roaring and the scratching ceased at once, and Tommy understood. The grizzly had been blocked in her hole by this monster rock that the landslide had brought down.

Chapter Five

A WORK OF MERCY

In the last few seconds, fear had been so vitally a part of Tommy that he cast it off slowly. He rubbed his faintly corrugated forehead. He dragged in great, consciously taken breaths. Finally he was able to step forward without trembling, but, at the first sound of his coming, another roar came thundering out of the prison of the bear, and again the big boulder shook as she threw herself furiously against it.

The savage threats made him stop short again, but one glance at the boulder reassured him. It must have weighed hundreds and hundreds of pounds, and, although it was so curiously balanced that the grizzly could thrust it back a little and make it shake, she could never really budge it.

Tommy came to the side of the rock around which the cubs had raced and saw that there was actually an opening a foot and a few inches across, covered with the scratches of the great brute where she had vainly tried to claw out a wider opening. Her roar had fallen to an ominous growling now, but Tommy, knowing that he was safe, went close and dropped upon his hands and knees to look in. A bear's cave is rarely very large, but this one had been made to order for bruin—a shallow place hollowed out of the living rock of the hill. Also, it faced south away from the prevailing winds, which is perfectly in accord with a bear's fancy. The heavy snows of midwinter must have covered the mouth of the cave

and given all the necessary warmth. Besides, she had dragged up some brush to close the mouth of the cave.

In a moment, the eyes of Tommy were accustomed to the shadow, and he saw all too clearly. There lay the great brute, with the hair worn from hips and flanks. Hair was worn around her shoulders and neck, also, where she had attempted to thrust herself out past the boulder, and there was fresh blood from her attempt of only the moment before. He saw her paws and marked that the claws were broken short or worn away by her efforts to dig through the rock. And her desperate, reddened eyes glared out at him.

As for the cubs, they had regained courage as soon as they returned to the neighborhood of their mother. They began to steal toward the opening from the little cave in order to examine the stranger more carefully, but the mother, with a deep growl, scooped them back with the flip of a forepaw and with a violence that rolled them head over heels. They arose, shaking their heads, whined a little, and then sat up on their haunches, their little forepaws dangling, their sharp ears pricked, and stared at Tommy with insatiable curiosity.

How his heart went out to them! Bear cubs could be tamed, he knew. He had actually seen a burly yearling chained in the yard of a mountain rancher. And he had heard old trappers tell tales of Adams, king of bear tamers, who had reared bears that fought for him against their own kind and served him as pack animals—even as hunting dogs! If he had those bright-eyed little fellows in the cavern yonder, what companions they would be!

He sat down with a sigh, cross-legged, and watched them and wondered, while the wise old bear rested her great head on the bruised, bleeding paws and studied him in a reserved silence, as though she realized that she had less to fear from this man cub than from terrible man himself.

It would be easy enough, Tommy decided, to lie in wait and capture the little cubs when they ventured out, but, if he had them in the cave, there would be nothing to feed them. That thick layer of fat that a bear accumulates to sustain it during the hibernation months still left the old mother enough strength to suckle her cubs and sustain herself, and it might be many days before she began to starve. Eventually, however, unless she were freed to forage for herself, she must die, and the cubs must die with her for the lack of milk.

All of this Tommy knew, and the problem weighed heavily upon him. How could his strength avail to move that rock or to widen the opening? Even if he succeeded, would he not be opening a way so that the great brute might rush out and tear him to pieces?

Still, tentatively, he struck the boulder with the back of the axe. It brought a stunning roar from the old grizzly, so that Tommy involuntarily shrank back, but also he noted that a flake of rock had loosened and fallen under the blow. Tommy studied the monster rock curiously. It was hard as flint in seeming and in fact, but it was so very hard that it was brittle. Its surface had easily defied the tearing claws of the bear, but it proved friable under the stroke of something harder than itself. In fact, as he studied it more closely, he saw that its base, where it had struck other rocks after the fall down the mountain, was powdered to dust.

He tried it again, and with a harder blow, and this time a larger chip was loosened under the impact of the steel. The mother grizzly advanced furiously to the mouth of her choked cave and reached out a long forearm toward him with another roar, but she retreated almost at once and lay crowded back so far as possible in her cave. And Tommy commenced his work seriously.

It was slow progress that he made at the best, for there

must be a huge portion of the rock worn away before the great body of the bear could issue, and all he could do with the heaviest blow was to knock off a thin layer, bit by bit.

There was no roaring from the grizzly now. With her ears sharpened, her head raised, she watched his movements as eagerly as though their significance had finally dawned on her, and Tommy at length ventured to carry his work to the very edge of the aperture that opened between the rock of the boulder and the rock of the mountainside. Now, if she could understand at all with her brute intelligence, she would appreciate what he was trying to do, for every flake of stone that he loosened was perceptibly widening the surface.

When his arms were wearied by the hammering, he scraped the rock fragments away and stood up to stretch the kinks from his back and legs. As he stood away, the mother lunged forward and sniffed curiously at the place where he had been working. Still she cuffed the cubs into a corner when they attempted to investigate for themselves, but her own fears had so far relaxed that she lowered her burly head to her paws and watched and watched with the reddened little eyes.

Tommy worked until his aching shoulders stopped him, and by that time the shadows were beginning to slope far east among the trees, so he took his last look at the bear family and bade them good night. A boy cannot do without names. He had christened the fatter of the cubs Jack and the slenderer one Jerry, so he called their new names to them and then picked up his axe and turned homeward.

Dusk began to gather as he walked, but still there was enough light for him to see and kill another grouse. It was between sunset and dark when he reached the camp with his prize.

Others had been there before him. There would be no

35

need of burial for the body of poor Billy. A scattering of bones was all that was left of him, and Tommy, shuddering, searched the ground and found the trails of great-footed timber wolves and small-toed coyotes. These had devoured the burro, and, led doubtless by their insatiable appetites, they had come to the mouth of his cave and had even succeeded in scratching away half a dozen of the smaller stones. They had been able to make no entrance, however, and Tommy felt a thrill of pride in his work of fortification. Utter fatigue, however, buried all sense of satisfaction. He could barely keep awake while he half cooked his dinner, and half an hour later, with the fire smoldering just outside the cave and his blankets made down within its mouth, he was sound asleep, to dream of weird monsters locked in caves from which he liberated them, only to have them fly at his throat. He did not waken until the sun was over the eastern mountains.

Chapter Six

STRENGTH TO PRESERVE

He rose like a conqueror, for had he not faced hard fortune, and in so short a space made a home, killed his own food, and cooked it? If there were sorrow just behind him, and unknown terrors in the future, he kept away from all thought of these things by centering his mind resolutely on what lay immediately before him. The first thing, even before breakfast, was to bury the bones of poor Billy. He shoveled a hole in the soft dirt, and in half an hour all that was mortal of the burro lay underground, with a litter of heavy rocks above it to keep out curious wolves.

Then he cut a slender sapling, straight as a rule and willowy in suppleness. To the end he tied the fishing line and hook. On the bank of the little stream that worked around the foot of his hill, he found bait in plenty at the first turn of his shovel, and soon he had jerked three big trout from the water.

That made a delicious breakfast, toasted brown over wood coals as he had been taught to do by John Parks. After he had eaten, he stood up and stretched his arms, filled with a sense of joyful power. How painfully small and weak his was, matched with those enormous mountains, those huge, dark woods. Yet he had won a livelihood from them these few days; he would keep on winning it until his blazed trails led a rescuer to his camp.

But, if he wakened hungry from the fasting of a single morning, what must be the case of the poor mother bear? He knew that after hibernation a grizzly eats little during the first week, but it might be many and many a day since the big bear had wakened from her season of sleep. She must be wild with famine and with thirst, he thought.

Close to the cave of bruin, the day before, he had heard the voice of a brook and even had seen the waters pooled in a little lake that promised to be brimful of fish. So he took with him for the day's expedition the fishing line and rod, his father's four-pound hammer, which was one of the most valued articles in the pack, the revolver tied on his hip, and a square of the tarpaulin on which their blankets had been laid. So off he went through the woods, with his whistle running thrillingly before him.

But no one can whistle long through the solemnity of virgin forest. The music died away, and Tommy went on, silent and serious, among the great trees. Now that he was left lonely in the wilderness, it took on a different face and spirit in his eyes. The shadowed places were full of a solemn interest.

The huge trunks were full of signs to him. Every tree carried a character of its own. Every rustling breeze seemed to hold a message for Tommy, if he could only have understood the sighing voices. Instinctively he walked softly, letting the toe strike first, and avoiding all twigs that might make a crackling underfoot. Now and again he paused, near a tree, and reconnoitered the forest ahead and behind. It seemed to him that the moving shadows must be cast by living beasts of prey, which stalked him. No matter if reason told him that they were not apt to rove abroad except during the evening and the night, still he was troubled, and he took care not to walk along the trail that he had followed the day before.

He reached the clearing with its litter of stones and fallen boulders, and, as he stepped out from behind the trees, he discovered that even his silent coming had not been silent enough, for there were the two little balls of fur, Jack and Jerry, scurrying as hard as they could for the shelter of the mother's cave. Their hair-trigger senses had warned them of his approach. When he stepped toward the cave, he was greeted with the same tremendous roar from bruin.

In spite of all he knew about her helplessness, that bellow of rage stopped him short and lifted the hair on his head with a prickling fear. But he went on again, reassured, and leaned over to look inside. At sight of him, it was apparent that the mother recognized her visitor of the day before, for she dropped down to the ground and laid her head on the forepaws once more, watching him with unblinking eyes. Yonder were little Jack and Jerry, standing up as gravely as any grown men could have done, with their forepaws folded across their chests and their sharp eyes twinkling out at him through the shadows. It was a thrilling sight to Tommy. His heart went out to them strangely, and he turned and hurried away toward the creek.

It was even better stocked than he had dared to hope. The first worm that wriggled on his hook had hardly touched the surface of the water when it was seized, and he snatched out a silver-flashing four-pounder. The little pond fairly swarmed with hungry life. In five minutes he had brought a dozen prizes to the shore. They lay flopping and quivering all around his feet, and Tommy laughed with the joy of the sport.

He had to make two trips with fish in his tarpaulin before he had brought all the prizes to the vicinity of the cave. On the second trip he found that mother bruin was standing up, her head wedged against the opening of the cave. She had smelled the fish, and she was wild with hunger, indeed.

Yet when Tommy came near with a fish in his hands, she

promptly drew back so far as the meager limits of the cave would permit, and, when he threw in the fish, she allowed it to flap within an inch of her nose without stirring to devour it. But there was a convulsive twitching of her nostrils, and Tommy knew that it had been eloquent to the scent of the great brute.

He tossed in another. Now she shoved her head forward, smelled the first fish, smelled the second—and even allowed Jack and Jerry to scramble up and do as she was doing. They sniffed the fish from head to tail, and then stood up and eyed their mother, plainly asking her what was to be done with these cold things whose odor was so delicious. Tommy threw in a third of his spoils, and now, as though the number of them assured her that they were untainted, the mother began to eat. Half a dozen went down her gullet as fast as Tommy could throw them in, and he laughed with pleasure at the sight of her evident satisfaction. But the seventh fish she cut in two and ate only half, and the eighth she did not touch. Plainly her stomach, still shrunk by the winter's fast, would not permit her to eat more. But Tommy threw in all the rest, and then went down to the creek and returned with a gallon of water in the tarpaulin. He poured it into a hollow of the rock near the mouth of the cave and watched her lap it up— but only a few swallows was all she wanted. The rest she allowed Jack and Jerry to come and wallow in, smelling it with their keen noses and then cuffing it tentatively with their paws, until finally they were tumbling and scuffling in the midst of it.

It was too great a temptation to Tommy. Little Jack stood nearest him with back turned, and with a quick reach and snatch Tommy caught the cub behind the neck and jerked it out.

It was the signal for pandemonium to break loose. The

frantic mother came to life with a rush that brought her crashing against the opening. The poised boulder quivered— then sank back into place. In the meantime, her roar was threatening to burst the ears of Tommy, while at the same time his hands were unbelievably busy with Jack.

The little bear was armed with tiny claws, sharp as the claws of a cat, well nigh, and with needle-like teeth. And instinct or scuffling with his brother seemed to have taught him how to use both weapons with professional skill. In ten seconds, blood stood out on a dozen little scratches on Tommy before he had young master bruin secured with a firm grip behind the ears, as a cat may be held. Then, realizing that to battle was vain, he struggled to get back to his mother, whining piteously.

But Tommy held his grip. The wild roar of the mother had subsided to a terrible growling, while, thrust forward so far as she could come, she watched every movement of Tommy with a grim anxiety. He was careful to remain where she could see his every movement. He began speaking in a low, gentle voice, as soon as he could make himself heard, and stroking the soft fur.

The whining of Jack fell away to a subdued moan of terror. At the same instant the uproar of the mother ceased entirely. It was as though she did not wish to make a noise that might take up some of her faculties and prevent her from noticing every touch of the boy as he handled her precious son. Finally she silenced Jerry, who was squealing still with a piercing insistence, with one of those flips of a forepaw that sent him tumbling and threatening to break every bone in his body.

But he rose, as always, in perfect unconcern, carefully wiped the dirt from his bruised nose with his paw, and sat up to watch the progress of affairs with greater care. That cuff had silenced Jack, as well. He no longer even struggled, but cowered down under the caresses of Tommy's hand.

He seemed to find a pleasure in the stroking, too. Finally he turned his head and dared to look his captor straight in the face. It was only an instinct that he met those strange, human eyes at such terribly close range. Then he jerked his head away. But the quiet, happy voice of Tommy, thrilled and delighted by his conquest, gave Jack new courage. He looked again.

There was no cuff to reprove him. The gentle stroking continued. The quiet, human voice that sent such mysterious currents of electric surprise and pleasure through the heart of Jack went on. Finally Jack ventured closer. He stood up on the leg of Tommy. He actually sniffed at the face of this harmless stranger who had such delightful powers.

The heart of Tommy leaped. He had not known until now how desperately empty his spirit had been, how completely full of loneliness he had been poured, but the sniffing of the trustful, curious little cub at his face brought the tears of happiness to his eyes.

He took the cub as before and ventured toward the mouth of the cave. The mother growled softly, and the ears of Jack flattened as he heard the voice. He was placed on the ground, and he crawled toward mother bruin as though he felt that he had been playing the errant against orders and must be punished for his transgressions. But the grizzly was only too happy to have him back. She licked and sniffed every inch of him, and then retreated with a growl of satisfaction to the rear of the cave, where she lay down as before to watch for the development of events.

It was all most mysterious to her. She had been taught by mother nature that all beasts take and hold only to destroy. But here was her helpless offspring taken away and then restored to her, safe and sound. Moreover, it had been taken by man, and she had learned from the wise mother before her that man is the one thing to be dreaded in all the range of the mountains. Nothing else could harm her. The stoutest mountain lion fled from its kill at her approach. All wild brutes trembled before her. But man, she had been taught, sees from afar and kills from afar—an inescapable death. Not in vain had she had her encounters with three separate packs of dogs with which she had been hunted, and, although she had escaped each time by miracles of cunning and endurance, she carried the scars of five bullets on her big body, and the bullets themselves in her flesh.

But if she had been taught some lessons by pain, she could learn still other lessons through the kindness of the new teacher. Bear and dog come from a common ancestor, and both have the power to understand the ways of man. Although she dreaded Tommy still because of the man scent which was so abhorrent to her, yet she was beginning to feel that, just as he was smaller than those other men who had trailed her, so was he gentler, also. And who could tell? If the others had strength to destroy, he might have equal strength to preserve.

At least she would wait and watch, and watch she did, with her great head tilted cannily to the side, wonderfully like a dog, while Tommy took up his four-pound hammer and renewed the attack on the rock that fenced her in.

Chapter Seven

FRIENDSHIP IS STRENGTHENED

He made wonderfully good progress with the hammer. The axe had been a clumsy tool for the work of the day before, but the shorter handle of the hammer gave Tommy a better chance. It was a heavy tool, to be sure, and, although he stood with braced legs and swung the hammer with a regular rhythm, yet his shoulders and back were aching before he had been at it long. But the rock was falling away in great and greater flakes. And now the entrance hole was perceptibly widened.

When he retired to scrape away the fragments, the mother bear came again to the opening, and now all of her broad head could pass through. She whined up to Tommy with understanding as he approached again.

When he sat down at the entrance and held out his hand, she did not at once cuff Jack away as the curious little cub started slowly to investigate the meaning of that inviting hand.

She allowed him, the first time, to come within a few inches of the hand, sniffing eagerly, before she knocked him away with a growl that warned him to stay out of danger and let well enough alone. But when Tommy persisted in staying there, she merely pricked her ears the second time and watched without interference.

For curiosity in a bear is almost as great as its fear of death. The strange sight of a forest fire had once held her fascinated

44

until a far-flung arm of the conflagration cut in behind her and nearly blocked her retreat. She had retired with a scorched back and a deeper respect for the great red enemy, but forest fires remained as interesting as ever to her. Now, much as she dreaded the small human in the mouth of the cave, she was devoured with insatiable curiosity as to what he would do if his hand touched her cub again. Once before she had seen Jack handled, and yet he had come back to her, rank with the man taint, to be sure, but safe and sound in body and limb. Might it not happen again?

It did happen. Little Jack came to the fingertips, sniffed them, ventured closer, shrank from the hand that attempted to caress him, and then came back and allowed the fingers to rub his head. He went farther out. With a faint growl of anxiety, she saw him taken up. But then there happened what had happened before. He was soothed by a gentle voice. He was stroked and rubbed to his heart's content. Even when those sharp little teeth of his closed on the hand of the boy, even though that bite brought a small drop of crimson to the surface of the skin, he went unpunished. Bruin was too amazed for thought. But she was delighted until her flanks quivered with the sensation. What could be a greater joy to her than to drink in these great draughts of knowledge?

To be sure, when Jerry attempted to follow Jack, she decided that one risk was enough at a time, and he was warned back, cowering, by a terrific snarl. But when Jack was returned to her a moment later, her examination of him was most cursory. At a glance, at a sniff, she knew that all was well with him still.

The work at widening the hole continued now, and Tommy made the chips of rock fly. But when the afternoon grew late and the spring sun sloped into the far west, he threw down the hammer with a great sigh and rubbed his aching shoulders as he contemplated what still remained to be done. It meant days and days of this labor—and his hands were already blistered with what he had done.

Yet what a wonderful thing it was, thought Tommy as he started home that evening, that it could be within the power of his small hands not only to support his own life in the wilderness, but to save the lives of three other creatures? And the sense of labor accomplished and other labor to be done toward the good end filled him with a solid self-respect that was new to him. He felt these things; reason was not yet developed in him to the extent of allowing him to be mentally conscious of them.

Once more he was too tired to keep his eyes open for long after he had eaten his supper, but, as his eyes closed in profound slumber, a new thought came to him. In the morning he would take all that he needed with him, block the mouth of his big cave with more and heavier rocks, and move to stay by the bear cave until the work of liberation was completed.

That promise to himself he kept when the dawn wakened him. How little he needed. Salt, a little flour, matches, and the rifle, the hammer, and a blanket tied up in the tarpaulin—that was all. As for the other food he required, his fishing line would get it for him, and he could supplement that excellent fare by knocking over one of the stupid mountain grouse now and again.

Few as the articles were, they made a heavy pack for the legs of a twelve-year-old, and he was panting before he reached the bear cave after his breakfast. It seemed that his particular scent was now well known, for there was no thunderous roar to greet him—only a deep, anxious growl. And the little cubs, playing as usual in the clearing among the stones, retreated only to the mouth of the cave and there stood up on their hind legs, as bears do, to observe him, until they were dragged inside by the paw of bruin.

But even this anxiety left her later on. She permitted Jack to steal out, during one of Tommy's resting periods, while he sat down, always taking care to be in view of the mother bear so that she could see all that happened. For his great care was to reconcile her to him. As for the cubs, a thousand other persons had tamed young bears, but how often had grown grizzlies been made into safe companions? So much the greater triumph if he eventually should succeed! If a boy of twelve could succeed, surely that would be a proof that kindness is a greater weapon than the rifle. He had heard his father say that, but at the time he had not been able to understand.

So he lay on one elbow near the mouth of the cave while Jack stole cautiously out to him—followed by an anxious growl or two, as though to warn him that he must be on his good behavior. But Jack observed caution only for a moment. He skirmished around Tommy for a little while, and then he came straight to close quarters for a better investigation. And there followed a wonderful game!

There were so many possibilities. There were pockets filled with strange scents that might be inquired into. There was the strange-smelling leather of the shoes, which might be chewed upon. And if one climbed to the shoulder of this playmate, his head was crowned by a thatch of hair just like the hair of a bear, although not quite so rough, perhaps.

By this time Jerry had played the part of an idle spectator longer than he could endure, and he came out for his share of the fun. Where one had broken the ice already, it was not hard for a second to follow suit. In five minutes Jerry was every whit as familiar as Jack, while mother bruin contented herself with crowding her head out the opening and observing each move.

With that romp ended, the cubs stayed out to continue

play of their own, while Tommy went back to his labors. At noon he went down to the brook and caught more fish, some for himself, but more for the grizzly, since she had devoured the last of those he had brought her the day before. He fed them to her, then brought up water as he had done before and actually ventured a hand inside the cave to scrape the dirt out of the hollow of the rock that served her as a drinking trough.

But bruin merely snorted at him and came to smell the rock after he had done with it. When the water was brought, she drank, long and deep. After that, there were new mysteries into which the cubs were quickly initiated. First of all, when Tommy's fire was lighted, they scampered, whining, back to the cave, but, after the flames had died down a bit, they were lured by the delicious odors of the roasting fish and ventured close again. They not only came close, but one at a time they sat up on their haunches and received tiny bits of the fish from the tips of Tommy's fingers. And they relished the taste!

Where one thing was good, why might not all be harmless? Alas, that it could not prove to be so. Poor Jerry selected for his next investigation a little, red-hot wood coal and, after a bit of tentative sniffing, picked it up boldly in both forepaws.

There followed a shrill squeal of pain—a roar from mother grizzly—and a slight taint of burnt hair in the air. Tommy turned anxiously to watch bruin. Would she feel that he had burned her young ones purposely? By no means, apparently. She simply sniffed the burned paws, and then promptly turned her head away and calmly ate another fish, as though she intended to convey that those who would not be warned must take the consequences. But that day and the next and the next, Jerry went about on his hind legs, or, if he wanted to run, he had to put all his weight upon the outside rim of his forepaws.

All those days Tommy was working like a Trojan to widen the mouth of the cave. A week passed, and he was still at it. And now he could no longer catch fish to satisfy bruin. In the first place, it was harder to take them in the waters of the creek. In the second place, and primarily, the appetite of bruin had grown beyond all measure. Both food and water she seemed to require in unheard-of quantities. He kept enough of the latter for her in the cave, but of the former he could not bring sufficient. Tommy worked with all his might to let her out so she might forage for herself.

It was terribly slow work, however. The edge of the rock had given way rapidly enough, but now as he came to the body of it, every inch added to the gap meant many hours of hammering. There was one great advantage, at least. The blisters had dried away, healed, and now his palms were growing callused. New muscles, too, had grown out on his slender young arms, so that the labor of wielding the hammer was far easier. Probably the stalwart arms of his father, swinging a sledge, would have battered away the rock in great chunks and freed the big bear within a short time. But he, with his lesser strength, could only gnaw at the rock face little by little.

Ten days of labor passed, and now, half a dozen times a day, bruin came to the entrance and strove to squeeze her way out, but the passage was still not big enough. She would retire and lie down to watch and wait, although sometimes, as the wind brought to her the delightful fragrance of roots and of honey from over the woods, she would raise her big head and growl with deep impatience.

In the meantime, there could be no doubt that even her brute mind understood perfectly the service that human hands were performing for her. There was not a growl when Tommy came near her. She would come close to the entrance to the cave and lie there, just out of range of the flying chips, and observe his work with keen satisfaction. He, on his side, did all that he could to push forward their acquaintance. When he came up with fish, now, she would crowd as far out as she could, her little eyes glittering with a ferocious hunger—for the appetite of a bear is the appetite of a pig— and Tommy would feed her the fish he had captured, one by one, from his hands. He ventured at first only by holding the fish by the tail and offering the head foremost. But he grew bolder day after day. His child's mind, having seen her do no wrong, could not conceive her repaying his kindness with beast ingratitude.

So, on a day, half closing his eyes, screwing up all the courage he could summon in his shaking body, he held out a small fish on the palm of his hand—and mother bear took it away at a bite without touching the skin of his fingers! She snorted a little. That was all. Then, as he kept the trembling hand extended, she licked the last trace of the fish oil from his palm!

It was almost the greatest event in Tommy's life. For a moment he sat back incapable of speech, his heart thundering. But a little dog-like whine of eagerness from bruin made him continue with the feeding, and from that time on every morsel she had was taken neatly from his hand.

Then—and all was ventured timidly, slowly—he tried to stroke that battered head while she ate. It was not easily done. At first, when the shadow of the hand extended over her, she winced away with a growl, her upper lip twitching back and disclosing huge fangs that could have shorn through the flesh and bone of his arm at a single snap. But, with twitching ears and quivering snout, she reached out for the fish again and this time allowed his hand to touch her head just between the little, pointed ears.

That was another great thrill, another great forward step of conquest for Tommy. Before the next day came, she was lying contentedly at the gap to her cave with Tommy Parks seated beside her—seated in fear, to be sure – stroking her great head and rubbing the loose fur, while mother bear seemed to take a profound satisfaction in his touch. But what was her pleasure compared with the wild delight of Tommy?

There he sat with two wild grizzly cubs playing on his knees, and with the huge head of mother bear dropped to the ground beside him. There he sat playing with the cubs, again, while that great head was raised and she sniffed at his back—a chill shot up his spine—at his arms and shoulders—at his neck—and snuffed strongly on his hair.

But that was all. No harm was done. Not once was her paw raised or were her teeth bared. To be sure, he knew that she had not admitted him to her confidence as the little cubs so freely admitted him, but she took him as a friend, an unmistakable ally, but for whose providence she must have starved and died there. And that, for the time being, was enough for Tommy.

Chapter Eight

A GREAT LESSON FOR TOMMY

What that two weeks of labor meant for Tommy, no one could have told—he, least of all. But for two mortal weeks he was so enthralled in body and spirit that he hardly had time to think back to the father he had lost, or to the strange and gloomy future. Or, if sorrow for the dead John Parks, or the dread of what was to come, now and then darted through his mind with a pang, the pain was short-lived. Weariness leaves not much room in the spirit for anything but itself and the longing for sleep— and a weary boy he was long before the closing of every day. If he were not weary, he was in the thick of his work or resting momentarily from it or sitting soberly beside the scarred head of mother bruin or romping wildly with the cubs.

They had grown prodigiously during the two weeks. One could hardly recognize in them the soft little balls of fur that Tommy had first seen. They had grown, indeed, like their mother's appetite, and that was the despair of the boy. They skirted here and there all around the clearing. A thousand things came to their senses—things that remained invisible to Tommy.

Sometimes, he would see them, of one accord, start digging the soft dirt where there was nothing on the surface, and presently they would be snuffing in the dirt like little pigs, and champing at white, soft roots. The strangely sensitive noses had told them that the roots, once found, would be good to the taste. Not that they actually ate any quantity of them. Mother's milk was their food, and would be for weeks and weeks to come, but they loved the taste of things, of nearly all things, so it seemed. They would chew grass or bark with avidity and eject it with equal disgust. An end of Tommy's coat was a morsel to be tested, at the least, as poor Tommy learned to his despair. They scratched at the bag that held his small and dwindling supply of cornmeal. And they persisted in coming after him and digging up the grains of corn that Tommy found in a separate bag and bethought himself to plant.

Finally, in despair, he had taken all that remained of that precious seed and carried it back to his own home grounds. There, along the banks of the little rivulet that flowed across his plateau, he planted the corn, with high hopes for what it might bring forth for him in the autumn.

But even his home place was not secure from these ready prowlers. They loved Tommy with a perfect and beautiful love. When he was absent, they wailed for him in unison. And, when he took his daily trips back to the home cave to see that all was well, to replace whatever stones had been scratched from the entrance by some prowler, or to open the cave and examine the condition of his total worldly possessions, the cubs formed the habit of following him some distance down the way.

At first they would turn and scamper back to the mother as soon as the distance made them uncomfortable or the tall woods oppressed them, or, most of all, the sullen commands of bruin herself overawed them. But every day they went a little farther until they reached a point when they were more afraid of going back alone than of going ahead into unexplored country with Tommy. So it was, to his unspeakable delight, that they one day went with him to the home cave.

They began to grow homesick and hungry at once, and they whimpered most of the way back to their mother, but, having followed him once, they could not resist the lure each succeeding day. They returned always to take a severe cuffing and scolding from bruin, but what little bear can remember a beating from one day to the next? Jack and Jerry certainly could not.

Bruin was wildly jealous at first, but her jealousy diminished. If Jack and Jerry depended upon the boy for fun and romping that she could not give them, she depended upon him for the very food that sustained her life, and, although her appetite was even more rapidly outgrowing his ability to supply her with provisions, a small oasis is better than a complete desert.

Moreover, the time of liberation was approaching. Little by little the solid rock had been eaten away by the hammering. Perhaps it was because he had gained strength from practice, perhaps it was because he had studied out little systems of attack, but it seemed to Tommy that the rock began to grow softer and to break away more and more readily until, finally, every stroke gave him a chip.

Yet he still thought that the hole must be far too small when, one morning after he had done a scant hour's work, bruin approached the gap and deliberately thrust herself through up to the shoulders. There she stuck, and, when she drew back, growling, Tommy attacked the rock with a freshened hope. He knelt in the entrance itself. He shortened his hold on the hammer, and the rock fell before him in chunks. Some of those fragments landed with cruel force on the head and body of bruin, but she refused to move back. With a fascinated interest she watched and held up a great paw to shield her face from the flying fragments, just as a man will shelter his eyes against the glare of sunlight.

Tommy laughed at her as he worked, and he worked until his trembling arms could not lift the hammer again. Then he stepped back. He was weak all over from the exertion. His head swam, his legs sagged beneath him; it seemed that surely he could never again attack that stubborn rock. Bruin, in the meantime, stepped to the gap, sniffed at the place where he had recently been hammering, with her head cocked wisely to one side, and then deliberately wedged into the gap.

At the first effort her shoulders came clear through. The head of Tommy cleared instantly. He forgot his weakness. Bruin, grunting with satisfaction, lunged forward again, and suddenly she was in the open, her sides scratched and bleeding, to be sure, by the sharp projections of the rock. But what did that matter, compared with the freedom she had gained?

Jack and Jerry, too, seemed to realize how great this moment was. They galloped before her and stood up and cuffed at her face with their little paws. But the grizzly, with a grunt and a growl, turned about and confronted Tommy. All the friendliness which she seemed to have felt for him while she was hopelessly imprisoned now vanished, apparently. Tommy, with a beating heart, stepped forward with extended hand, speaking softly. But she stopped him with a warning snarl, a terrible, indrawn breath, showing those great, yellow fangs as she did so.

The next instant she had wheeled and was ambling swiftly away toward the familiar shadows of the woods. Jack and Jerry scampered in her rear. In another moment she was lost in the undergrowth. The cubs turned and whined at Tommy as though bidding him follow, also, but a deep-throated growl from the front made them turn about and scurry away. In scarcely a minute from the instant of her liberation she was gone, and Tommy stood still and listened to the diminishing crackling of the twigs. He stood still, and the tears trickled slowly down his face, for, after all, he was only twelve, and this desertion was more than he could stand.

The keen, steady heat of the sun burning through the shoulders of his shirt roused him at last. Labor had swollen his hands with blood. Long labor had weakened them. It seemed to Tommy that he had barely the strength to gather up his belongings and make his pack again. When he had started on the back trail toward his cave, he was so weak that he had to sit down for a rest every two or three hundred yards.

It was a melancholy march, indeed, that trip back to the camp. He felt in a single rush the reflex of the excitement that had been supporting him for the past two weeks. The old sorrow, the old fear that had been lurking in the back of his brain all that time, now stepped out and took possession of him. Again and again the emotion of self-pity came so stingingly upon him that the tears welled up into his eyes.

He fought them away. He forced himself to raise his head and to step on more lightly, for, if he gave way completely to the weakness, he felt that it would overwhelm him in a wave of unbearable strength. But how changed everything was. All these days he had been walking gaily back and forth along this trail. He had come to know each runlet that crossed the way, each clearing, each denser growth of trees. All had become familiar and kind to him by constant seeing, but now the familiarity was gone. The trees wore altered faces. The wind swept through the treetops with an ominous strength.

A chilling thought possessed him. He had been so confident that his blazed trails would soon lead a trapper or traveler to him, and a full two weeks had passed without a sign of a deliverer. Might not the entire summer and autumn pass in just that manner? In such case, what would he do when the bleak winter dropped upon this country, when the snow fell many feet in depth, and when the cruel northers howled around the peaks and cuffed the forest until it groaned? How strongly that wind blew, he could see evidenced on every hand. Yonder was a tree with a broken top. Here was a mighty pine knocked over simply because it had stood by itself in an exposed place. How dark and cold and cheerless the cave would be through that long, winter season.

The heart of Tommy was failing him completely, and, as always when he was sad, the picture of his dead father grew up in his mind as vividly as if John Parks were walking just behind him—as if at any moment he would hear the familiar voice, feel the hand dropped upon his shoulder.

He built strange fancies, kind and cruel at once. He imagined John Parks returning, weak and pale, with a tale of how he had been carried down the current, battered and torn by the sharp rocks, but how he had managed to reach the bank— how he had lain, delirious and sick, for days—how he had managed to kill a grouse, perhaps, and so obtain food. And so, at last, he was come back to Tommy. All the horror was simply a great, gloomy adventure.

Such thoughts came to Tommy as he walked home this day. Before he reached the clearing, there was established in his mind an undying hope that once again, before the end, he would find John Parks.

The minds of children move strangely. Delicate, small things that quite escape the attention of their elders, to them are all in all. A tree in the dark of night may seem to them ominous as the victim of the play; a smile may shock them through and through with happiness; a frown may lock up a lasting sorrow in their hearts. However cruelly casual they may be themselves, they are keenly aware of all the moods of others. To poor Tommy, lost in the wilderness, every mountain head that reared above the Turnbull valley was as dreadful as a threatening man about to descend upon him or holding a threat of perpetual danger above his head. So he took this weird hope for the return of his father into his inmost soul, and it cheered him wonderfully. It was like the flame of a match cherished painfully in a wind—the last match of a store, lighted precariously. So it was that he kept that thought of his father apart in a quiet place of his mind to be turned to in moments of dread and sorrow.

All was well in the clearing. Other prowling beasts of prey had been there, to be sure, drawn by the odor of the strong bacon, perhaps, or lured by the man smell where there was no man. The rocks at the entrance to the cave had been partially scratched away. But no harm was done.

Tommy removed the stones and found all well inside the cave. That night he had not the courage to go abroad foraging for food. He let the very squirrels chatter unheeded in the trees above his head. He ate bacon and fried cornmeal and went to bed hopelessly, wearily. His last thought before he closed his eyes was of Jack and Jerry. What merry, merry companions they would have been for him. But now they were gone forever from him into the wilderness, and, when he encountered them next, they would not remember him. All that he had done for them had been thrown away.

Chapter Nine

COMPENSATIONS

There were dreadful times ahead for poor Tommy, but, of all that was to come, nothing so stayed with him, nothing was so burned into his consciousness, as the fortnight that followed. Yet it should have been an easy time, for the spring was softening toward summer. All the forest stirred with life. Within a hundred yards of his home cave there lay an ample hunting ground for Tommy. He had no need to range abroad in search of game. It came up to his doorstep, so to speak, and invited the hand that destroyed it. Yet he grew thin and anxious. For one thing, an almost straight diet of meat is not good for a child, and although long walks through the forest hardened him, and the labor of cutting down trees and chopping them into firewood seasoned his lithe, young muscles, still, as he grew harder, he grew thinner. And worry was the poison in his life, the worry of loneliness.

A boy overflows with talk. He is full of questions as a pine tree is full of needles. But all this chatter of light-hearted words and inquiry was dammed and stopped up in Tommy Parks. He began to develop a deep wrinkle in the very center of his forehead, a wrinkle that should not have come there for another twenty years.

Every day was a long agony of waiting—for what, he could not tell. But something must happen, something must flow into the sterile current of this life. That expectation took the form of hearing his father in every echo, his breath in the whisper of the wind among the trees, his footfall in the crackling of every twig, and sometimes Tommy would draw himself up with his small fists gripped, so keen was the suspense.

Sometimes, too, he felt his brain whirl, his eyes grow misty, as the strain began to tell upon him. Every day was an eternity. It made no difference what he attempted to do. Thought came between him and the labor of his hands.

There is always a saving grace of some kind. For Tommy, it came in the form of the sprouting of the corn that he had planted. In the rich soil of the sunshiny bank of the stream that trickled across his little tableland, the seed germinated quickly and then the pale green shoots came feebly above the surface of the ground. Once up to the light, they flourished amazingly. A dozen times a day, Tommy went out to watch them growing, and, when he sat at the mouth of his cave, listening and waiting for the men who must someday come to find him and save him, the play of the sun glistening upon the waving young stalks was a perpetual delight to him.

Every young plant took on a different character in his eyes. There were some that prospered more than others, of course. There was one that was the dwarf, the weakling. Tommy felt a keen affinity for it. Finally he discovered that it was being crowded by a small rock on either side, and, when these were removed, it began to prosper like the others—or even more so. There seemed to be a greater energy in it, born of repression. It shot up noticeably every hour, so to speak. Tommy was delighted by it. Although he kept the ground loose around all the others, that particular stalk he tended with an extra precision.

It was at the end of that miserable fortnight of silence and dying hope, just after he had lain down in his blankets at the mouth of the cave, that a new adventure came. He had closed his eyes and turned on his side toward the cave when he heard a light, crunching sound on the gravel of the small plateau. That little sound was enough to bring Tommy into a sitting posture, fevered with hope. As he jerked upright, a great growl turned his blood to ice.

Six feet from him, a great grizzly reared up with dreadful arms raised, ready to strike. Through the twilight, and looking up, it seemed to Tommy that the monster was as tall as the trees. He could not stir. Then, from behind the big bear, two little cubs came running to him, tumbled upon him, rolled him over, licked his face, bit at his hair, with a babble of noise and a flurry of many motions.

Tommy got staggeringly to his knees, with a wriggling cub under either arm, and he saw that the great bear that had loomed so ominously above him the moment before had now dropped upon all fours and was digging busily for an unexpected root near the entrance to the cave. The family had come back to him!

Tears of joy started into the eyes of Tommy. He rolled the cubs gaily in the dirt. He boxed them on the ears and was soundly cuffed in turn. For a wild half hour they played. Then Tommy built up a great fire to celebrate the occasion, and the two little bears came close—staying near his side, since he was the fire master—and sat back on their haunches like two, bright-eyed little boys to watch every dart of flame, every leap of the fire.

They had been taught many of the mysteries of the wilderness in that last fortnight, but nothing their mother could show them rivaled the miracle of that living thing which had no life, that fluttering and whispering thing which blossomed out of harmless wood and had a sting which would rankle for hours in the tortured flesh.

It was not fascinating to the cubs alone, but to the mother

bear as well. She, too, came close. She, too, decided that safety lay in being as close to Tommy as possible. She, too, reared back on her haunches and sat up and grunted with satisfaction and unending surprise as the fire warmed her.

That stomach had been hugely rounded since Tommy last saw her. How many grubs, what quantities of white roots, what millions of ants and bugs, what rabbits, what stalked birds, what hordes of honey, had poured down that insatiable gullet since she started out on her hunting expedition, Tommy could only vaguely surmise. But in the two short weeks she had put herself in excellent condition. The scars of the battering to which she had subjected herself in her efforts to get out of the cave were almost concealed by the fur, although here and there was a place naked of hair.

What she had become since she went back to the wilderness, Tommy could not guess, but now, when he stretched out his hand, she jerked her head quickly around to him, to be sure, but she made no indication of suspicion. She even grunted with loud pleasure when he rubbed her behind the ears.

Even the joy of a fire to watch could not take all of the attention of the cubs away from Tommy. Now and again they would steal bright little glances at him, or flick a paw toward him, as though to make sure that he was not gone.

A strange, strange picture, the four that sat there around the fire, bathed in the light, with the great circling darkness behind them. But before long the strange odors wafting from the interior of the cave to the sensitive noses of the bears drew them in for a tour of inspection. Tommy took the last, lean remnant of his bacon and the flour and placed it on a high ledge at the side of the cave to which even the agility of the cubs could not attain. And, although mother bruin reared up and stretched as high as possible toward the fascinating fragrance, she soon abandoned the hopeless effort and went around examining whatever she could find. All was thoroughly probed by three acute noses, each of which was strongly attached to the memory of a separate bear, and, when this was done, the bears were sleepy and curled up within the radius of the firelight.

But Tommy was so happy that he could not sleep. If he drowsed now and again, he was quickly awake. Every time he wakened, he had to step over and see how the three reposed. Each time he came near, the watchful mother opened one eye and grunted recognition of him. Every time he looked at them, they reminded him more and more of dogs—wiser than any dogs that ever lived, and a thousand times more powerful, of course—but stiff, very dog-like in their ways. And every time he looked at them, the more Tommy realized that life with these companions would be possible.

He fell into a sound sleep just before dawn, and he was wakened finally by Jack and Jerry tumbling upon him at the same instant. It was a bright morning, with the pink hardly gone from the horizon, and all the snow-topped mountains more beautiful than Tommy had words to describe.

He made a quick tour of the dozen bird traps that he kept scattered at favorable places near the home cave, and he came back with half that many prizes. Five of them went to Mrs. Grizzly; one was enough for him. While he cooked and ate his own portion, he was consumed with laughter, watching the mother eat while the cubs played with the flying feathers.

Yet she had finished her five long before he had consumed his one. She sat by and licked her chops enviously while he ended his meal, but, to the surprise and wonder of Tommy, she made no effort to take the meat from him by force. Indeed, he had noted before that she had respected him always, as though she had been duly impressed by the strength that had worn away the imprisoning rock and loosed her.

After breakfast, she showed signs of uneasiness and a desire to make off, and Tommy noted them with a failing heart. But at length he decided to wall up the mouth of his cave and, when she left, go on a trail with her. That, in short, was exactly what he did. Hurriedly he tumbled the stones into place, while Jack and Jerry scurried to and fro, sniffing every stone as he stirred it, and making absurd efforts to imitate him. Jerry, in fact, managed to pick up a stone between his forepaws and waddle gravely along with it and drop it in place; Tommy laughed and his sides ached at the sight.

Mother bruin, before he ended, was on the farther side of the clearing, calling to her youngsters impatiently. So the whole party started out to explore, going straight up the hillside. They set a pace for the first mile that Tommy found hard to follow, but at the end of that time the mother slowed her steps. She went slowly, slowly, her nose on the very ground, and Tommy thought that she must be getting the beginning of an important scent. But, when he ran up to her, he found that she was following a thick stream of ants and licking them up carefully as she went.

Chapter Ten

ALONE ONCE MORE

The sight of such a diet gave Tommy a qualm of the stomach, but mother bruin seemed to relish that food immensely. Jack and Jerry, incurable imitators, hurried to join in the fun. Here and there they went, sticking their noses into the train of ants, licking them up, and then ejecting them, to the huge amusement of Tommy, until finally the big bear decided that they were in her way and promptly called them aside.

As always, they pretended that the cuff and tumble had been exactly a part of their plans. Just where they fell, they arose, without a whimper, and began to dig eagerly for imaginary roots. Then both stopped at the same instant and looked keenly at Tommy as though to ask whether or not he had understood. Although he had understood perfectly, he swallowed his mirth—just as he would have done had they been boys of his own age and as keen-witted as he.

The old mother, in the meantime, had come to the end of the ant trail, which terminated in a great hill of newly turned dirt covered with ants. Here she sat down on her haunches. It seemed to Tommy as though she were embarrassed by the riches that were presented to her. But not *Madame* Grizzly! Presently, with a rake of her claws, she opened the hill to its center. Behold the black swarm of the ants! Those that adhered to the bottom of her paw, she promptly licked off. Then the wet paw was laid in the midst of the hill again until the active ants swarmed thickly on it again—when it was raised and cleansed with a few swipes of the long, red tongue. So the game went on until the ants ceased to swarm—hundreds, thousands had been demolished by every stroke of that great tongue. Tommy felt that he had just witnessed the destruction of a great nation.

Now she rose and went on through the bushes, but presently she stopped and veered sharply to the left. It was an old, rotten log that attracted her attention. A tug with a forepaw turned over a weight that a grown man could not have budged. *Madame* was instantly busy, to the horror of Tommy, in eating the fat, white grubs that were exposed.

Truly this was a varied diet! Who would have expected such a monster to pay attention to such small details of her table? But on she went, inveterate scavenger, and presently picked up and gobbled at a mouthful a dead bird—then on again, following the guidance of that matchless nose.

Tommy felt that he was being truly initiated in the ways of the wild.

They dipped into a hollow, in the center of which a streamlet had created a small bog, and here *madame* diverged from her course for the sake of wallowing in the soft, cooling mud. She came out again, shook herself with a vigor that sent the mud flying in all directions, then started up the farther slope, pausing here and there to rip her way down to roots and devour them, then swaying on with her clumsy stride, which covered such an amazing amount of ground.

The strange thing was that the cubs could keep pace, but it seemed to require no particular effort of them, whereas Tommy was completely winded before the first hour had ended. Something must be done. A roll in the grass had cleaned the mud from bruin's back, and that suggested an expedient to Tommy. He approached her, when she was starting on after a slight pause during which she had ripped a rotten log to pieces and hunted for grubs inside it, to small purpose. When he dropped a hand on her back, she stopped short and swung her great head around. And when, cautiously, he slipped onto her back, she shrugged her shoulders and shook the loose skin so violently that he was promptly knocked on the farther side.

He got up a little bewildered and found her turned about, sniffing him curiously. Once more he tried the experiment, and this time she allowed him to sit astride her without objection. So, strangely mounted, up the slope they went together, swinging on at a gait that covered the ground with an amazing rapidity.

The heart swelled in Tommy. Surely he was the first who had ever been able to mount so strange a charger! To be sure, once or twice she paused and swung her head back at him with a growl of annoyance, but on the whole that burden was too small to impede her, and finally she went on contentedly. When she paused to dig for roots, or when she scented a woodchuck and began to claw through the dirt to rout the little fellow out of his hole, Tommy slipped down from her back and stood aside to watch. But, when she climbed on again up a slope, he resumed his place at her back. There was no objection.

For one thing, food was coming the way of bruin thick and fast that morning. New scents, mingled scents of food trails, were crowding upon her. Besides, there was deeply engraved in her mind the memory that he had fed her when she was helpless. Freedom and food, the two main essentials of existence, had come to her from his hand, and even the brute intelligence of the bear could not forget.

That was the first of a hundred expeditions with bruin. During the hundred days Tommy felt that the bear must have covered easily thirty miles a day, in spite of all her pauses. She was a tireless traveler, rarely breaking out of her ordinary, scuffling walk, but swinging on at an astonishing rate, even in that walk. An unending hunger urged her to continue that journey so long as she remained unwearied. But weariness seemed to be no part of her make-up. Tommy saw her once work a whole hour digging out a woodchuck on a mountainside, tearing out the loose stones and standing up and piling the stones with her paws as deftly as a man could have done— stones which a man could not have budged. So, tearing out the stones and piling them, digging out the dirt with her powerful claws, she worked down until she had moved a carload of heavy material—and the reward of all that tremendous labor was a single little woodchuck wriggling out of the dirt— a single mouthful for the big bear.

But it was food, and every mouthful of food was worth working for. Tommy learned something from that—something to stir his gratitude. Wise and patient forager she was, it took a day's work to supply her with provisions, but he, at a stroke, could supply himself with a meal. There was one serious impediment. He could not carry a gun with him when he went trailing with bruin. If he carried the revolver, she would permit him to attend, but he could not ride her up the hills. The scent of the detested steel would make her rear up, growling terrific threats, if he attempted to come too near. So he left the gun behind him. All he carried was matches. During the day, it was usually possible to rescue part of a rabbit from the grizzly after she had surprised one. It sometimes angered her, to be sure, but Tommy learned to pick his time, and, if it were after she had been foraging long and successfully, she did not seriously object if he purloined so small a part of her spoils.

He took the fishing line with him, also. In fact, that provided some of the choice fun for Tommy, for, when they came to a promising stream, or to a deep, silent little pool, *Madame* Grizzly sat back on her haunches so far from the edge of the water that her shadow would not fall upon it. Then she would call her cubs to her with ominous growls. Sometimes, she would gather them to her side with her strong forelegs, strangely like a human mother would use her arms, and, when all was reduced to silence, she would turn with a pathetic eye of expectation to Tommy. At once he became the hero of the hour.

He would choose his place, attach the line to a small, light rod that he usually carried with him, and drop it into the pool and await results. With what keen anticipation they all watched. Yet, when the fish came shining out of the water, there was no stir on the part of *madame,* and, if the cubs dared to move, she brought them back with a bruising blow of her great forepaws. So she waited until a fish was thrown to her, although, as a matter of fact, Tommy never had the heart to keep the first fish away from her. But she would sit there and gobble a dozen at a time, as fast as he could throw them to her. Great hunter though she was, she had no skill to match against this human cunning. It was small wonder that she now and then allowed this ample provider to take part in her own kills.

In fact, their partnership was perfect. There was only one thing to spoil it, and that was that *madame* was prone to sleep during the middle of the day, and to hunt morning, evening, and in the night. But even to these habits Tommy accustomed himself. After all, cubs need sleep, and, by sleeping when they did, he secured rest enough. He learned to drop flat on his back in the shade of a tree, throw out both arms, and fall instantly to sleep. Five minutes later, he could wake up at the first, silent rising of *madame* and go with her over some arduous trail, running beside her over the level or downhill, and riding on her back when she climbed a slope.

He learned many things during that hundred days. In the first place, he discovered the limits of *madame's* domain. He had always supposed that a grizzly wandered where she would up and down the mountains, but, in this case, he learned that *madame* had boundaries that she never crossed. The eastern limit was the timberline of those bald mountains over which Tommy had climbed. The northern boundary lay beyond several ranges some thirty miles from the Turnbull River. The Turnbull itself was the south line, and the western extremity of her province was about fifty miles from the timberline of the bald mountains down the valley of the Turnbull. That magnificent region she covered in a surprisingly short space of time. To be sure, it consisted of some 1,500 square miles of ground, but *madame* was doing her thirty miles of travel every day, and soon Tommy had seen her cross and recross every bit of her province.

He learned the territory as though a map of it were printed in his mind. He knew every pond, every stream, every mountain and hill. He knew the big trees, the aspen groves, the thickening hedges of lodgepole pines where they climbed the upper ridges, the open places fit for a roll and a romp with the cubs.

The cubs, meantime, were waxing big and strong. When they stood up on their hind legs now and boxed with him, he was soundly beaten. With doubled fists, with keen eyes, with dancing feet, he would circle around them, dealing blows as swift and hard as he could, and they, for a time, would miss, or pretend to miss him, but, when they decided the play had gone on far enough, one lightning and inescapable flick of a forearm would stretch him on his back with a bruised chest.

It was rough play, but the whole life Tommy was leading was rough, and he had grown hard as nails. A grown man could never have adapted himself to such living, but Tommy was just past his twelfth birthday now, and, at twelve, mind and body are almost as fluid as water and will take any sort of shaping. So long as Tommy was happy, he could stand anything.

He was happy, riotously happy! He was beginning to give up hope of being rescued by a traveler this summer or autumn—but the rescue could be put off until the winter and the height of the trapping season, he told himself. Even if someone came, they would hardly have found him at the cave, for he was away from it sometimes a week at a stretch. Besides, what mattered the future? Tommy was twelve!

The autumn came, drowsy with mists, and then chill of nights. His precious corn had grown up, and the ears had turned into maturity and been plucked and laid away in the cave for future use, laid high on a shelf of rock, while Tommy vowed solemnly that no hunger should reduce him to the necessity of eating them, for he knew that, if he stayed in the valley another year, that corn meant bread to him.

Autumn passed then, and in early December the day came when *Madame* Grizzly began to lose her appetite. Tommy was prodigiously worried, but both mother and cubs seemed to be interested in nothing but sleep. Every day was worse than the preceding ones. They were irritable, also, and did not wish to be bothered by his attentions, and finally *madame* began to dig a cave. Tommy knew that she was preparing for the winter's sleep.

She selected a spot among the northern mountains, a hillside that faced the south. There, under a thick matting of roots, she made her excavation. She dragged in a quantity of long, dried grass and shrubs. She assembled more brush at hand, and on a day she retired into it, followed by the cubs, and choked the entrance by drawing in brush after her. Tommy found himself once more left alone.

Chapter Eleven

THE GREAT ACCIDENT

It would be late in March or early April before she came out again, he knew. In the meantime, the long white winter had begun in those upper mountains, and Tommy must prepare for a life in the snow.

Yet his heart did not completely fail him. He knew the country in which he was living, he told himself, and he would manage excellently. For one thing, he had laid in a store of nuts during the late autumn. They would help him through the lowest periods of the starving winter. For the rest, he still had ammunition, and it would go hard if he could not keep himself in food. If he could have foreseen what was coming, he would probably have lain down and resigned all hope at once. But providence spares us too much foresight.

His clothes were in tatters, but, as the cold increased, he began to wrap a blanket around him when he went out to hunt. Inside the cave he managed very well. He noticed on the roof of the cave a small section where roots grew down and it made him guess shrewdly that there was a considerable gap in the rock at that point. So he climbed up with the shovel and dug down through the dirt until, to his delight, his shovel struck through into empty air. When he had finished his digging, he had uncovered a hole of rugged outline, two feet across, in the center of his roof. That became his chimney. To be sure, a fire of wet wood or green wood would fill the cave insufferably with smoke, but on the whole the draft worked very well. Usually he had a brisk, bright blaze that kept the cave comfortable, while a thick blanketing of smoke gathered in the top of the cave and slowly poured out through the opening.

So furnished, he could defy the cold, and, when the wind stood in the south, he needed only to block the entrance to the cave with stones. Of course, there were vast, empty stretches when he was neither eating nor sleeping or hunting or cooking. But those periods he filled quite comfortably with reading only two books that John Parks had put in his pack. Two books make up a small library, and these two could hardly have been better chosen for Tommy. There was a Bible, and there was a copy of Malory, both sadly battered by the packing, but both still readable. To Tommy they were inexhaustible treasures. Malory he knew before in fragments. Now he devoured it whole. As for the Bible, he had felt it to be a great and dreary book fit for old women and Sunday, but, when the conversation-hunger drove him, he opened it perforce—and was suddenly lost in talks of old wars, wild vengeances, strange prophecies, inspired men. There was much of it that he could not follow easily, but he found long passages that were solid entertainment, and many and many a long hour he spent tracing out the words, one by one, with the motion of a grimy little forefinger.

Grimy Tommy certainly was. Suppose a close look is made of him on the day of his tragedy, that fatal accident that nearly snuffed out poor Tommy's life. Hunger wakes him. He sits up in the dim twilight of the winter and the cave combined. He lights a fire, groaning and shivering in the cold. The rising tongue of yellow flame shows first a ragged mop of long hair, partly standing on end and partly falling down across ears and neck. He is huddled in a blanket that for the moment covers his body. The firelight gleams on a berry-brown face, thin, with the cheeks, which should be rounded by childhood, as flat and straight as the cheeks of a grown man. His eyes, sunken under frowning brows, glitter with the firelight; keen, blue eyes as restless as the eyes of *Madame* Grizzly herself.

Now hunger rouses him. He stands up and goes to the nearest shelf of rock and takes from it two frozen fish, for yesterday he had broken the ice of a pool and had caught several prizes. But suddenly the thought of fish makes his stomach and throat close tight in revolt. He throws them back on the shelf. He steps into a pair of huge shoes—an extra pair of John Parks's shoes, for his own had worn out that summer. He winds the blanket as deftly as an Indian chief. He goes to the entrance of the cave, rolls a stone back, and steps out onto the crackling, hard, frozen surface of the snow.

There he stands, breathing deeply of the fresher air, the color leaping up into his cheeks. He is a tall boy for his age—some three inches short of five feet, big-boned, with the promise of great hulk when he is matured—if he may live to maturity. But nine months of solitary life, solitary work and play in the wilderness, have hardened him like leather. The muscles of those lean, long arms have surprising strength.

He looks about him upon a white world. All the mountains that step away north and east and south are sheeted like ghosts. The plateau is thick with snow, which has blown here and there into mounds and drifts. The level branches of the evergreens are pressed down by thick layers of the heavy snow. A keen wind is blowing. It takes edges of the blanket and tugs them straight out. It pries through the loose folds of the cloth and sends its icy teeth through and through the slender body of the boy. But Tommy only shrugs his shoulders and steps out.

Yonder he enters the forest. Here the walking is better, for he does not have to wade to his knees through the snow. He needs only to pick a course where the trees have sifted the snow to the side, and where the ground is covered with only a thin layer. But, even so, now and again he steps into a little hollow up to the waist. In half an hour he is wet and freezing cold. But still he shrugs his shoulders and sets his teeth. If he lives to a happier day and a greater strength, the world will have to pay him a heavy toll for all this pain.

Now he stops short. His keen eyes have seen three little humps of snow and ice thrust up on a branch halfway to the top of a tall tree. He stands watching them intently, making sure. These are three young partridges, he is sure. They have roosted yonder in the early winter. Snow has covered them in a night. The warmth of their bodies has melted the nearest snow, so that it touches them in no place, and the heavy frost has frozen the outer layer of the snow to an iron-hard consistency. And so their winter house is made.

While he stands there, motionless, his eye catches on something white as the very snow, and moving like an arrow across its surface. It is a weasel, that fierce little wolf that preys on all small life. It darts past almost across his feet, so intent is the terrible killer on the blood trail across the surface of the pure snow. Instantly he is gone. Tommy looks after him with an involuntary shudder. Then he is into the branches of the tree. No matter that those branches are slippery with ice, no matter that the deft feet of Tommy are burdened with those great, oversize shoes; he is climbing to make a kill, and he will not slip.

Up he goes. He lies out on the branch, twining his legs around it. He crumbles the first icehouse. Yes, he was right! He wrings the neck of the poor bird and drops it to the ground, and so with the next, so with the third. But the third is smaller. He will carry it down with him. So he thrusts back a fold of the blanket and stuffs it into his coat pocket. Suddenly he thrills with fear. In that pocket are the matches, and they must not be moistened by this wet body.

He jerks out the bird again, and behold! down through the air flutters a whole drift of matches that have adhered to its damp feathers. The sharp wind catches them. They blow away in a cloud and disappear among the branches of the next tree.

Poor Tommy! His heart stopped when he saw that dreadful mischance. He dropped the partridge unheeded. He thrust his hand into the pocket—not a match was left!

For the moment, he lay there, half stunned by his fortune. All he can see now is how small was that fire that he started to build before he left the cave. Down the tree he drops like a veritable monkey from branch to branch. He falls from the last one upon his face in the snow. But that is no matter. Neither do the precious birds matter to Tommy. Off he started, racing through the snow. If only the fire will last until he reaches the cave.

But he has come much farther than he dreamed. It seems that he would never be able to cover the distance between. At last, with burning lungs, with blinded eyes, with the blood pounding in his head, he rushes into the mouth of the cave and finds that the floor is black as night. Not one spark of the fire has lived!

Above it he stands, sick and stunned. There are the small branches lying in a little circle, with their center portions burned away, until they were out of touch with one another, and so the flame died in the cold air.

Tommy sinks down upon the sandy floor and presses his hands over his face. This, then, is the sentence of death. On raw meat he might live a little time, but without fire he must surely perish.

Chapter Twelve

HEAVEN-SENT HEAT

The miserable days dragged on, and he still lived. He managed, by heaping all the blankets and the tarpaulin upon him, to keep warm enough in the cave so long as he was lying down, but, when he moved around, the cold ate into him venomously. If he had had the proper food, he could have endured well enough, but raw meat was more than his stomach could stand unless he were exercising vigorously, and in that bleak weather he dared not expose himself for long at a stretch. Gradually his strength diminished. A great drowsiness began to grow in him. It spread through his body first—an aching fever, a false warmth broken with fierce spells of shivering and utter cold. Then it reached his brain, so that he wanted to do nothing but lie still all the day in the heap of warmth-giving stuff that he had piled up.

But, even in his drowsy times, there was an anguish of hunger, a craving for food that he could not have. He found himself wasting with a terrible rapidity. His body grew emaciated. His cheeks sunk. His hands, when he raised them, were wasted to a point that he hardly recognized them. Yet, everyday, in spite of that diminishing strength, he forced himself to get up and go into the great outdoors to see if he could sight some animal, some beast of prey, that he might kill with a rifle bullet to clothe himself in the pelt.

Once he sighted a great timber wolf, but his shaking hands could not hold the weapon firm, and the bullet flew wide while the wolf trotted out of sight with the slowness of contempt for this puny hunter. He failed thus, on the only occasion when he sighted a pelt worth having. Now the time came when he went out more and more seldom. Finally for three successive days he did not leave the cave.

It was only a sudden reflex of will that drove him out at length. He wakened one afternoon from a stupor. He hardly felt hunger now. A haze hung before his eyes. The same haze hung over his very mind. But there was a sudden parting of the veil as he saw his hand raised before him, a mere, withered claw rather than a hand.

The horror brought him erect. There he stood, shuddering in the cold and realizing that, when he lay down again, it would be to fall into a sleep from which there was no waking. Fear drove him on more strongly than dread of the cold could keep him back. Presently swathed in blankets, he staggered weakly out of the cave. A side draft of the wind caught him and knocked him flat. He rose again and went on blindly through the forest, the rifle dragging down in his hands as though it were of a ton's weight. He knew that, even if he saw a fur worth having, he could not shoot the wearer, and yet on he went, driven simply by a horror of the cave and the death to which he would be returning if he went back to it.

He found himself stumbling across a raw, bare patch of earth from which a recent landslide had torn the trees and shrubs. Tripping on a loose stone, he fell headlong for the tenth time. He was stunned by the fall. When he roused again, he found that he was half frozen, so frozen that, when he leaned and picked up the gun, the weapon fell from his numbed fingers and, striking a rock, knocked out a bright spark.

Tommy stared with vague agony down at the stone. In the very rock there seemed to be fire. He alone in all creation was without warmth. He was still half dazed, half stupid, but that spark had fascinated him. Regardless of the harm that might be done the barrel, he dropped the rifle again, and again the spark jumped from the piece of flat, black stone.

Suddenly he picked it up with a wild hope growing in him. Sparks will light fire. This must be a flint. What had the Indians used for centuries before him? With the stone hugged to his breast, with the rifle trailing behind him, he made on toward the cave as fast as his weak knees would support his strides.

So, muddy from his falls, with a ringing as of bells in his ears, he entered the cave and looked about him for tinder. He found something excellent for his purpose—a pile of dried bark that he had used to start his fires while the matches lasted. Some of this he shredded to a bundle of small fibers, so brittle that they threatened to crumble to a powder. He gathered larger wood nearby, and then he took the revolver, as a handier bit of steel, and, the flint dropped at an angle, he began to knock a shower of sparks upon the tinder.

They fell all over the bark. A faint smoke arose, but, when he ceased striking the flint, the smoke died out. He worked until his weak arm ached. Then, as despair was coming over him, there was a new thought. He hammered again with all his might and main, tossed aside the battered gun as soon as he saw a small spot glowing on the bark, and began to fan this with his breath.

He blew till his lungs threatened to burst, till his head grew dizzy, and, behold, the smoldering spot of dark grew in width, ate into the bark. Hastily he placed more of the shreds of the crumpled bark upon the spot. Again he blew. Now a thin column of smoke rose. To Tommy it was the most blissful sight he had ever seen. Literally it meant life!

Again he blew with all his might. The smoldering increased, grew audible. There was a faint sparkling, the smoke cloud increased tenfold. He began to fan the heap with a part of the blanket. Now the smoldering place became a vivid orange that lighted up his hands at work. Suddenly a little tongue of flame shot up, quivered, while Tommy hung breathlessly over it, and then steadied into a swiftly growing blaze. He had made fire! He had made it of steel and stone and wood! A great wave of gratitude flooded through Tommy. He cast up his arms. Tears streamed down his face.

But he dared not wait. Quickly he threw on the bits of wood. The smoke rose again as the fire worked. Then a new and stronger flame burst out. Like a madman, he threw on more and more wood. A roaring blaze shook up toward the top of the cave. A soaring flame licked against the roof itself. Tommy sat down with his blanket thrown away, unneeded, his arms put out to the heaven-sent heat.

A month later, on a day, there blew up a warm wind. It was a true Chinook. It melted the snows in the lower valleys as though a fire had been built upon them. In a fortnight Tommy had dry footing for his hunting trips.

He came out from the winter prison, hollow-cheeked, still weak in body from the great ordeal, but full of pride, full of invincible confidence in his strength to face any ordeals before him.

Chapter Thirteen

THE STRANGER COMES

He made his first trip to the cave of *Madame* Grizzly. The entrance was still blocked with brush. He exerted no effort to rouse them. He was wise enough to understand that there is no safety in interfering with mother nature when she is at her work.

So he went back down the slopes, finding every trail crossed with rivulets fed from snows that were melting under the trees. It was on this trip that he made his first kill of big game. Something stirred in a thicket before him. He jerked out the revolver and stood eagerly waiting, and in a moment a little, brown-bodied deer stepped into view, and Tommy fired.

He almost regretted what he had done as he stood over the beautiful little body a moment later, but life in the wilderness is a grim thing. It is kill or be killed, and Tommy had lived there long enough to understand it.

Many times he had seen his father cut up deer. Now he set busily to work getting off the hide. There was many a slip of the knife, many a slit in the tender pelt, but eventually, after a weary task of tugging and pulling and cutting, the work was done after a fashion. Then he cut the deer into quarters, hung three parts as high as he could on a shrub, and carried one ham back to the cave.

To roast a quarter in the Dutch oven was a considerable task. Moreover, it was one that he had never performed before except under the strict supervision of his father. It was dark in the cave before he peered at his cookery and decided that it was done. What a fragrance greeted his nostrils as he opened the oven! Surely that was worth waiting for.

He had just sat back to enjoy the meal in prospect, when a human voice, the first he had heard in almost a year, spoke from the entrance.

"Hello, son."

He leaped to his feet with a shout of astonishment. He saw that a big, rough-bearded man had just crawled through the entrance to the cave and had risen to his height—a huge, thick-shouldered man in the later middle of life.

There was one pang of disappointment, of unbearable sorrow, in Tommy as he saw that it was not John Parks come back to him. In that instant, hope of his return died forever in Tommy's breast. In another breathing space, he was wild with joy because a human being had at last crossed his trail. The long silence was ended. He went to the big man with a rush.

"Oh," cried Tommy, "how did you come . . . how did you come? How did you find me?"

Here the big fellow stepped back from him, gathered his bushy brows, and peered down at Tommy with little black, bright eyes.

"Look here, son," he said, "you ain't telling me that you're living here alone, are you? Your pa ain't here with you?"

He said this with an eagerness that Tommy could not understand, and the boy told all his story in ten words. But, the instant he had learned that John Parks was dead, the stranger seemed to lose all interest in the rest of the narrative and the story of Tommy's sufferings. He strode forward, lifted the cover, and inhaled the fragrance of the roasted venison.

"We'll eat now," he said, "and we'll talk things over later on."

So saying, his big knife instantly slashed into the vitals of the roast. He began to eat wolfishly, and Tommy, amazed and bewildered by such treatment, stood for a time in the offing. When he approached to take something for himself, the stranger lifted his eyes with a silent glare, and Tommy retreated again. Not until the big man had ended his meal, bolting the meat in great chunks, could Tommy take a portion in what he considered safety.

By this time he was thoroughly frightened, but the black-bearded fellow had reclined against a stone and spread out his legs toward the fire. He began to roll a cigarette.

"Make yourself handy, son," he grunted after a time when the cigarette was lighted and he had blown a cloud of smoke upwards. "Get some wood on that fire."

Tommy moved as though he had been struck with a whip, half choking on the mouthful he was eating. After he had obediently heaped on the wood and the flame was soaring, the fear of the taciturn stranger had increased in him to such an extent that his throat closed and he could not speak. He sat watching and waiting uneasily. Still the stranger did not stir, but seemed to drink up the heat of the fire, while his eyes bored into Tommy.

The boy began to notice the equipment of the big man now. He was wearing enough rough clothes which were plastered with mud and torn with a thousand small rents, such as come when one rushes recklessly through dense forest or climbs over rough rocks with many a slip and fall. Also, in spite of the bushy beard of the man and his stalwart frame, Tommy saw that the upper part of his cheeks were sunken and his eyes buried. Plainly he had made a long and hurried march. He had made it on foot and he had made it without so much as a blanket. Yet he had chosen to carry a perfect arsenal of guns and ammunition. He was weighted down with a Colt and a heavy cartridge belt crammed full of bullets, and now there rested beside him a repeating rifle of the newest and most expensive model. Tommy could see that it had been scrupulously cared for. There was not so much as a scratch upon the wood of the butt.

From these things he began to make deductions actively. Men did not travel over the mountains hastily in the time of the thaw, equipped with only guns and bullets, unless they were either pursuing or fleeing. And something told Tommy that this was not a case of pursuit. Men who pursue are fearless, and the keen eyes of this fellow rested upon even a boy like Tommy with a world of suspicion and cautious reserve.

"Look here, kid," he said suddenly, "how long have you been here?"

"Almost a year," said Tommy.

"A year!" said the other. "And nobody ain't been near you all that time?"

"Nobody," said Tommy.

"Not a soul, eh?"

"Not a soul."

The big man drew a great breath, and then, in silence, he stared off into vacancy. Presently he began to smile. Evidently what he had learned had pleased him immensely.

"And," said Tommy, "I'd like to know when we start on."

"What?" said the stranger. "When we start on?"

"I . . . I thought," said Tommy, "that you'd take me with you when you went."

The other laughed with a brutal abruptness.

"Now, why," he said, "are you aching to get back to other folks? What'll they do for you? Nothing! Look at the way I been treated by everybody. Look at the way everybody has treated me."

He stopped suddenly and eyed Tommy in that keen way he had, until he apparently decided that there was nothing to fear. He shrugged his shoulders. His tongue loosened.

"There ain't no justice down among men," he said in a voice half gruff and half whining. "They don't give a man a chance. Look at me! Is a gent responsible for what he does when he's got some hooch under his belt? No, he ain't. No right-thinking man can say that he is. But I wake up with a headache, not knowing what I've done, and find about a dozen of 'em chasing me with dogs and guns. No questions asked. They just open fire when they sight me. Well, says I to myself, what's all the fuss about? What have I done? But there ain't any use waiting to get my questions answered with a slug through the head, so I foot it for the hills and give 'em the clean slip and have a damn' hard trip . . . and finally I wind up here. And here's where I'm going to stay, and here's where you're going to stay!" he added fiercely. "I ain't going to have nobody sneaking out and telling where I am. If you've been here a year without nobody finding you, I guess I can stay here a year the same way. By that time things will have cleared up a little, and I can go down and look around and see how the land lies. Ain't that sense?"

He seemed to be speaking to himself more than to Tommy, and the boy kept a discreet silence. Suddenly the head of the fugitive jerked around, and the keen little brute eyes glared at Tommy.

"Come here!" he roared.

Tommy came, trembling. The big hand of the stranger shot out and clamped around Tommy's wrist. The pressure seemed to be cracking the bones.

"You're going to stay right on here with me, kid!" he thundered. "Besides, if you can forage for one, you can forage for two. So you start in and make me comfortable. And there ain't going to be no getting away. If you try to run for it, I'll start out and trail you, and I'm the out-trailingest man you ever seen. I'd run you down inside a couple of hours, and then I'd tear you to bits."

His eyes snapped, and his teeth gleamed behind his beard as he spoke. Tommy's heart turned cold.

"Speak out!" roared the big man. "Tell me how you like me."

"Fine," stammered poor Tommy. "I . . . I like you fine."

"You lie!" cried the big man, and with a sweep of his thick arm he knocked Tommy flat on his back.

The sting of the blow on his cheek worked like a strange madness in Tommy. He had been accustomed to the gentle ways of John Parks. He could not understand a rough voice and a heavy hand. Unreasoning, he came off the ground like the recoil of a cat and flew at the face of the stranger.

The latter had barely time to erect a guard, and that guard was insufficient. He lurched to his feet while the stinging, small fists were cutting into his face with a rain of blows. Once erect, he pushed Tommy away with a long, extended arm. The wonder left his face. A cruel interest took its place. He poised his great right hand.

"I'm going to lesson you," he said savagely, drawing his breath in with joy at the prospect. "I'm going to give you one lesson for the sake of manners and showing you who's the boss. Stand off, you imp!"

The last word was a grunt of rage as Tommy slipped under the extended arm and struck savagely into the body of the big man. Then the blow fell. It came straight and hard, with the overmastering weight of the stranger's shoulder behind it. It struck Tommy on the side of the head and rolled him along the ground. He lay there stunned with a sting along the side of his face and a warmth that told him that the skin had been broken by that brutal stroke.

"Get up!" roared the big man, and he kicked Tommy with his heavy boot.

That wild anger leaped into the heart of the boy again. He came off the ground, how, he could not say, and sprang into the face of the stranger.

"You little wildcat!" gasped out the big man, and recoiled, although driven more by astonishment than by his hurts.

That instant of recoil, however, gave another opportunity to Tommy. He leaped to the pile of dried wood that he had heaped along one side of the cave, and a second later the billet cracked heavily along the sconce of the stranger. Again Tommy struck, and again he shouted with a wild satisfaction as he felt the wood bite, soft and heavy into flesh. Then the stick was torn from his hand. He leaped away, and he raced for the entrance to the cave, knowing that now nothing could save him but flight. The big man was not cursing, and his silence meant strangely more than oaths.

Tommy was almost at the entrance when something told him to dodge. Down he dropped in a heap—and barely in time. The scooping arms of the big man swept over him, brushing his clothes. The toes of the stranger's boot lodged with sickening force against his ribs. Then the other crashed against the rocks with a shout of pain and rage. But Tommy, rising hastily to his feet again, knew that his finish had come, for now the big man was between him and the mouth of the cave!

Chapter Fourteen

THE WORK OF MAN

He slipped back into the very center of the cave where he would have more room. Yet he knew that even there he was playing a losing game. In speed of foot, in endurance, he could not compare with the grown man. Presently he would be cornered, and the great, bone-breaking hands would fall upon him. After that. . . . His horrified mind grew blank. But, having picked up another stick of wood, he waited. He might strike and dodge at the same time and so gain another chance to get at the outlet. But that chance was only one in ten. He glanced longingly up the side of the cave where he had laid away rifle and revolver on a higher shelf. Oh, fool that he had been to put his weapons in a place where they were not instantly accessible!

The stranger seemed to have the same thought. He had risen slowly from the ground, drawing out his revolver as he did so. But a second of thought seemed to reassure him. He pushed the Colt back into its holster. He began to advance slowly with such a face of fiendish rage that Tommy was paralyzed. No, there would be no dodging now. This cold fury would prove inescapable. He saw a tiny trickle of crimson down the face of the man and into the beard. That red mark would be warrant for his own destruction, beyond a doubt.

"Now," gasped out the other, "now, we'll try something!"

He came with his great arms spread out, moving with long, stealthy strides as though he were stealing up on an unwatchful victim. In that nightmare horror Tommy could not move.

It was then he saw a dark form emerging out of the spot of black night at the mouth of the cave. With Jack and Jerry crowding behind her, in waddled *madame* bruin with as much assurance as though into her own cave. A shout of joyous welcome, a cry of wildest relief burst from Tommy's lips.

That shout made the big man whirl on his heel. One instant he stood petrified with astonishment. Then *madame* reared up and stood immense on her hind legs, with a roar at this unexpected stranger. Another moment and she would have taken to her heels. But the big man did not wait. He plunged to the side of the fire and snatched up his rifle and pitched the butt into the hollow of his shoulder. It happened all in a twinkling. The gun spoke, and *madame* pitched heavily forward and died before she struck the ground.

There was a hoarse shout of exultation from the man. The rifle steadied again, spoke again, and Jack, with a squeal of agony, whirled around, doubled up on the ground with the pain, and then stretched out, limp. There stood Jerry, bewildered, sitting back on his haunches in the most utter amazement and looking to Tommy as though for explanation of this strange catastrophe.

Tommy's fear for himself was forgotten. He saw the gun steady. But he sprang at the big man, and the shock of his body made the other shoot wild.

"Curse you!" cried the murderer, and with a short arm blow he struck Tommy to the ground. "Your turn comes last!"

"Run, Jerry!" shouted Tommy as he lay in the dirt.

But Jerry did not run. His brain was not what it would be a day hence. It was thick and sleepy from the long hibernation. And calamities had rained down so fast upon those around him that his keen mind was stunned. He sat up there still with his head cocked to one side and innocently faced the rifle.

So much Tommy saw with a side glance, and he saw, too, that the big man was steadying the rifle for another shot, steadying it carefully. Thereafter, he would tell how he slew three grizzlies with three shots in as many seconds.

But fear for Jerry raised Tommy. He stood up with a shrill cry. Only with a gun could this destroyer be stopped. He reached for the butt of the revolver at the big man's thigh just as the other, with an oath, struck him down again. He fell, but his fingers had gripped the weapon and drawn it forth. There he lay with black night swirling around his brain.

"I'll brain you!" thundered the big man, and reached for the weapon that Tommy had stolen.

Tommy pulled the trigger. He fired blindly. All before him was thick night. In answer to the bullet, a crushing weight fell upon him, and he felt that he had failed. After that the darkness was complete.

When he wakened, Jerry was licking his face.

He sat up with his brain still reeling. There lay the big-bearded man on his face, beside him, motionless. In the entrance to the cave lay *madame* and Jack, in the same postures in which they had fallen.

That sight was enough to bring Tommy to himself. He stood up and ran to make sure. It was not the human being for whom he felt concern. It was not dread for having taken a human life that stung Tommy. It was overwhelming remorse that the affection that had brought *madame* bruin to him had brought her to her death.

She was quite dead, and Jack was dead beside her. He took the great, unwieldy head in his lap. Jerry sniffed the cold nose, and then looked up with a whine from the face of his young master for explanation. But Tommy could only answer with tears. Then, in the midst of his grief, he shook his fist toward the inert form of the killer. Here was man at last, man for whose coming he had yearned so bitterly. This was the work of man!

Chapter Fifteen

AFTER YEARS HAVE PASSED

The first minute of waiting is always the longest. That first year in the valley of the Turnbull was always the longest to Tommy. It seemed to him that it embraced more than half of his life, for fear and loneliness and weakness and peril had lengthened every day to an infinity. But the time that followed flew on wings. Every minute was crowded. There is no dull moment to the man who tears his living by force of hand and force of cunning out of the wilderness. And when events happen most swiftly, time seems to fly on the strongest wing. To Tom Parks it seemed that there was only one stride through the next few years. So let us step across them in the same manner, with one step, and come to Tom in the spring of his sixteenth year.

A babble of sharp noises wakened him, the daybreak chorus of the forest. Tom rose from his bed on a bearskin thrown across soft pine branches. He stood up, now grown to his full height of a shade more than six feet, equipped with nearly a 170 pounds of iron-hard muscle. He looked four years more than his sixteen, except that the down of manhood was only beginning to darken his upper lip and his chin. But that crease of pain and thoughtfulness that had been cleft in the center of his forehead had never departed, and there was a resolution, an independence of a grown man in his face.

He stretched his arms, long and powerful, until the last of the sleep fled tingling out at his fingertips. He yawned and exposed a set of white, perfect teeth. Then with a shake of his head, he tore off the shirt in which he had laid down to sleep. It was made of the softest buckskin, sewed with sinew—a roughly made garment with mere holes for the head and the arms. His trousers were of the same stuff, ending in a ragged fringe between knee and ankle. He dropped them from him and stood naked in the chill of the morning air—brown as though carved cunningly out of bronze.

Through the cave he sped into the rosy flush of morning sunlight, then, a flashing form, he was down the slope to where the creek swirled into a deep, long pool. He leaped onto a rock and stood a moment before plunging in. Around him, he heard life waking in the woods. He heard birds calling. He heard swift rustlings that were not of the wind among the foliage. Far above him a hawk flew. He marked its flight with interest. No, it was not a hawk. It was a great eagle. A hawk, at that height, would seem far smaller. Yes, it was an eagle—no doubt that old eagle of Bald Mountain. Tom Parks turned his head to watch until the speeding king of the air was shut from view past the treetops. Then he lowered his head and dived.

The water closed behind his feet without noise, with hardly a ripple. Silently he came to the surface again, turned on his face, and swam with long, strong, silent strokes straight ahead. It seemed that he would surely strike the great trunk that shot out from the bank, with its tangle of drowned branches. But, when he was a foot away, up flashed his legs, down went his head. He was under the trunk, then came, all noiseless as ever, to the surface, trod water until he was exposed to the breast, and stood there, laughing silently.

But that water was snow fed, ice cold. Even the leather skin and the tough muscles of Tom's body could not keep out the chill from vital places. Back he turned for the shore. The long arms slipped through the water. Without a splash he came to shore.

The sun turned him to a figure of gleaming, running quicksilver. But that wind, blowing on his wet skin, was too cold. He slicked the water from his body with his hands. Then he picked a section of clean grass, lay down, and rolled in it. He came up drier—and dirtier. He brushed off the leaves and what dirt would come. For the rest—what did he care? Dirt meant nothing in the life of Tom Parks. He wrung the water out of his long, sun-faded brown hair, and then raced up the slope to the cave.

Still he was not dry enough to dress. Many a day of stiff muscles and an aching body had taught him that it is better to have a dry skin before clothes are put on it. So he stepped to the side of the cave where a huge grizzly lay asleep. Into the side of the monster he thrust his toes and jabbed the ribs under their layer of thick pelt and fat.

Jerry awoke with a grunt, blinked, and then straightway stood up. He had grown into a monster even of his monstrous kind. There was well over a 1,000 pounds of meat and bone and hide in this giant; there would be even more when the autumn nuts had fattened him.

He put out his arms like a man stretching. But, the instant he did so, Tom Parks was at him. The hard shoulder of the youngster struck the breast of the bear. The long, brown arm wrapped around the furry body. With all his might he strove to topple Jerry. Topple half a ton's weight of heaven-taught wrestler?

Jerry merely grunted. With one bone-crushing hug he squeezed the breath out of Tom's body. Then came a flick of the forepaw, and Tom Parks was sent staggering to a distance. He gasped, but he came in again with a rush. His flying fists struck home on the solid body—one—two—but again came that inescapable stroke of the paw. It was nicely judged—oh, how delicately managed! A little more, and he could have caved in Tom's chest with the stroke, but Jerry was an old hand at this game, and he struck just hard enough to knock Tom flat on his back.

He was up again, like a cat, but that had been enough boxing for one morning. He was in a glow of heat, and the blood was coursing strongly through his arteries. He brushed off the sand, stepped into his buckskin suit, and slipped moccasins onto his feet. He was ready for the day.

Jerry went out to hunt for grubs on the hillside while Tom kindled a fire. Over that fire he fried flat thin cakes of corn-meal mixed with water. No meat till night for Tom. He had formed that habit long ago. But when evening came he would eat enough for three.

That quick breakfast done, he went out down the hillside and, with a shrill whistle, brought Jerry after him. Down they went across the plateau where that year's crop of corn was burgeoning out above the ground.

Jerry roved in the rear. He was an incurable loiterer. There were thousands of foot scents blowing to his nostrils every instant. He had to stop a few minutes here and a few minutes there to demolish a colony of ants or to turn a log and get at grubs or to tear a rotten stump to pieces because of the horde of insect life it harbored. Besides, he could overtake the master at will, for on one of these roving expeditions after amusement Tom loitered through the forest, seeing and hearing and learning out of an inexhaustible book.

When there was an expedition to a distant point on hand, that was quite another matter. Then one sharp, shrill whistle apprised Jerry that there was business on hand, and he forgot his appetite until the point was reached. But what he much preferred was one of these leisurely scouting trips. They might be back by night. They might not return for a week, for he had noted that Tom took with him the fishing line as well as his hunting knife. As for a gun, his store of ammunition had been used up long before. But the line and hook were enough, and, if he wanted additional food, he knew a dozen sorts of food traps that he could make and bait with good results. As for fire, he carried a piece of flint and the barrel of the demolished old Colt revolver. He could raise a flame when he willed.

Jerry did not sight Tom again until noon, and then he came up to the youth lying prone on a bank of grass and peering around a tree trunk to watch beavers busily at work cutting down trees. It was a new dam near the mouth of one of the Turnbull's tributaries. The water had been backed into a little gorge, and the beavers were just beginning to levy their toll on the forest. A dozen saplings were down and trimmed of branches, and Jerry stretched contentedly beside Tom to watch the work. To be sure, beaver meat was good, very good, and there was always an unfilled corner in that capacious belly of his. But now the little fellows were laboring so close to the edge of their pond that it would be impossible to surprise them. And, next to eating, Jerry loved to satisfy his curiosity.

It was a whole long hour before Tom had gazed his fill. Then he stood up and clapped his hands, and he laughed silently and heartily as the beavers dived for shelter beneath the water. He had learned his noiseless swimming from them, but he could never match their craft in water ways. But there was something worth knowing—this new dam. It was another treasure added to his horde. In the winter he would come down here and get enough fur to clothe himself like a prince through the season of the snows.

All the rest of that day Tom headed leisurely westward

down the valley of the Turnbull. Jerry followed, although in high discontent, for, by the evening, they had passed the limits of the territory over which Jerry's mother had roamed, and which Jerry and Tom had taken as their natural domain since the death of the wise old grizzly. But, as evening came, a windfall came to Jerry in the shape of a fat buck.

There had been born in Jerry the skill of all grizzlies in slipping silently through a forest, in spite of their bulk. So it was, gliding through the twilight, that he came suddenly on the rank scent of meat and an instant later—for they had turned directly into the wind—the deer sprang up before him in a thicket. Confusion made the poor creature run into the jaws of destruction. A crushing blow smashed its skull, and both Jerry and Tom dined in state that evening.

With the morning, when Jerry was preparing to turn back, hugely uneasy at this venturing into unknown country, Tom persisted in holding straight on down the valley. What moved him to it, he did not know, but, in this wandering down the course of the Turnbull, there had awakened in him a sudden and fierce disgust with the cave and everything in it and all the delightful country that he called his own. There was no temptation to go back over the bleak mountains that he had climbed with his father, but a hunger of curiosity grew up in him to see what undiscovered country lay westward.

Already he had come farther west than ever before, and still the pangs of curiosity increased, and he went on. In spite of the careless mode of travel, they had covered a full thirty miles the first day. On the second, the distance was a great deal more, for Tom pushed on relentlessly from dawn to midday. Then he rested, and both he and Jerry slept. But in the evening they pushed on once more.

So it was that they came to the first settler's cabin. It was almost dark, but far away Tom heard a faint, ringing sound that he presently recognized as the blows of an axe, clipped home with great force into hard wood. The sound ceased before he came close, but it was easy to continue to the place, with Jerry leading the way with an acute nose.

So they reached the verge of a man-made clearing. There was an acre of naturally cleared land. And there were ten acres more that had been cleared by cutting down the trees. In the exact center was a small log cabin whose open door was flooded with light and shadow flung in waves from an open fireplace. A guitar was tinkling and thrumming from the interior.

The heart of Tom leaped within him. The wind blowing through the trees above him was suddenly as mournful as a human sigh. Big Jerry, as though smitten with a sudden dread, turned about and looked Tom squarely in the face to read his thoughts. Perhaps it was only because the sensitive nose of Jerry was telling him tales of bacon and ham and a score of other delectables, and he was silently wondering why the master did not proceed to investigate.

But now the music ceased, and a great, rough, bass-voice spoke. It made the very hair on Tom's head bristle as he recalled that unforgettable voice of the man who had killed Jerry's mother. A man with such a voice could not but be an enemy made terrible by the possession of firearms.

In the gathering night, he turned from the house and made a gesture to the grizzly that sent the latter into retreat. But it was not to be an altogether peaceful journey. A shifting of the wind had blown their scent to the house, and suddenly, behind them, came the yelping of dogs, sweeping closer, then breaking with a confusion of echoes through the forest as they entered the trees. Jerry stood up with a profound growl to listen, while Tom, realizing that they could not flee from these fleet-footed assailants, planted himself beside the bear with a drawn knife.

Instantly they came—four huge, wolfish beasts, scarred with many a battle. They recoiled at the sight of the man. But on the bear was the scent of this man, and the bear scent was equally on the man. Their minds were instantly made up, and they flew to the attack. Two leaped at Jerry from the front. But they were wise fighters. They made only a pretense of attack. The real work must come from those in the rear. The other pair, trained fighters that they were, jumped to take the bear at disadvantage, and here it was that they encountered Tom.

His heart was raging with excitement, but he had learned that first great lesson of the wilderness, where all creatures fight to kill, that successful battle can only be waged with a cool head. Half crouched, ready to leap to either side, he poised the long knife. One brute rushed for his legs, and the other drove at his throat. He leaped high to avoid the first and, twisting to miss the second, he slashed it across the gullet as it flew by him.

He himself landed heavily on his side. He twisted to his feet like lightning. The dog he had used the knife on was standing to the side, head down, coughing and bleeding to death. But the first brute, wheeling as it missed its rush, was on him in a twinkling. The eye could barely follow the moves of Tom then. He sprang like a cat to the side, caught the great brute by the scruff of the neck, and, as the animal whirled to sink its teeth in his arm, he drove the knife home between his ribs.

His arm was bloody above the wrist as he turned back to Jerry, just in time to see one of the dogs, half wolf and half mastiff, venture too close. A lightning blow of the forepaw and a crushed skull for the dog were the result. The fourth dog leaped back, viewed the carnage for an instant, and then fled in dismay, howling.

Jerry made a lunge in pursuit, but Tom called him back, for voices of excited men were sounding not far away, and men meant guns, and guns meant that the only safety lay in flight. A low whistle apprised Jerry that overwhelming odds were now opposed to them, and Tom took to his heels.

Chapter Sixteen

A MISTREATED DAY

He ran like the wind during the first quarter of a mile, weaving deftly through the trees, for he had been trained to such night work by many a prowl in company with Jerry. He could read the ground underfoot almost as though he saw in the dark. After that first sprint, as the voices died away behind him, he still ran on like a wild thing that cannot measure danger but only knows that it is somewhere in the rear, an indescribable thing. His swift and easy stride did not slacken until ten miles were behind him.

Then, breathing hard, but by no means winded, he went ahead at a brisk walk, with Jerry lumbering and grunting behind him. They encountered a steep hill. He slipped onto Jerry's back, and they went up it handily. Down the farther slope they ran again, and so they hurried on through the night.

Just before dawn, he paused at a creek and spent an hour fishing with great results for Jerry and himself. Then they pushed on until mid-morning, reached the forested crest of a hill, and there made their covert.

They slept soundly until mid-afternoon and wakened as they had fallen asleep—in an instant. They climbed on, then, to a higher range of hills to the westward, and here, from the naked summit, Tom found that he was looking out on more than he had dreamed of.

Far to the east, Bald Mountain was lost in the pale horizon

haze. All that he could see was the procession of rolling, for-ested hills that climbed up the valley of the Turnbull. North, behind him, rose higher hills, climbing to naked mountain heights. South stretched the wide expanse of the valley, with the broad Turnbull flashing in the midst and sweeping away to the west in lazy curves quite different from the arrowy little stream that he knew near the cave and through his own terri-tory.

Westward, also, lay the things which most amazed him. In this direction the air was free of mist, the hills sloped away to smoother forms, and he saw the landscape dotted with houses and checked in loose patterns with fences. And yonder, not quite lost to his view, the houses collected in a vil-lage, a thick cluster of roofs and trees.

For years all of this had laid hardly more than a hundred miles from his own cave! He would have welcomed that sight four years before. This prospect would have been better than a promise of heaven to the lonely boy. But that was before the big stranger came to the cave and engraved in his mind the lesson that men are dangerous, treacherous, cruel, un-grateful. So it was that Tom, as he stared down on these houses, shivered a little and then cast a glance back over his shoulder as men do when they are in fear.

All his past, before the death of his mother and the day his father left the city and started into the mountains, was lost behind a veil of indistinctness. But he remembered enough to know that his father and mother had both suffered at the hands of other men, that there had been poverty in their household, that there had been hunger even. So there was in-grained in his mind the belief that men are evil. The first man he had met since the death of his father had repaid food and shelter with brutality. The second voice he had heard had been of one who kept fierce dogs that had attacked him without warning, without justification. In his buckskin trousers there were still spots of blood. Aye, that was the cardinal sin of man—bloodshed!

He shuddered in a strong revulsion.

Yet, that afternoon, in spite of Jerry's earnest endeavors to stop the westward journey and head back toward the home country, he insisted upon skirting along the hills to get a better view of all that the valley might hold. Before the day was ended, he saw another proof that man is brute, and nothing but brute.

They passed among the trees to the head of a promontory, a low plateau that thrust out into the more level or rolling ground, and from the brow of this eminence Tom found himself in view of men—many men. A ranch house with shambling barns and outhouses around it had been built just beneath the cliff, and now, between the rearmost of the houses and the base of the cliff, a dozen men were gathered with their horses, in or around a large corral. Several of the men were grouped closely around one of their number who lay upon the ground, apparently badly hurt. They were pouring water upon his face and chest. But he was not the main object of interest.

In the center of the corral four men were holding a young bay stallion, saddled and blindfolded. He danced restlessly, his head snubbed to the saddle of another horse. Instantly Tom connected that empty saddle on the bay with the prostrate man outside the fence.

Presently the latter arose and staggered to the fence, where he leaned feebly. Another rider now advanced, climbed into the saddle, and the others grouped as closely as possible around the fence to watch while the ropes were taken from the stallion and his head was freed of the blindfold.

There followed one minute of more condensed action

than Tom had ever seen, even when Jack and Jerry were having a mimic combat, for the bay began to leap into the air, tie himself almost literally into a knot, and then land on stiff legs. The rider was jolted and jarred from side to side. Suddenly the bay reared and flung himself backward. The yell of the watchers came tinglingly up to Tom on the height. But his fierce heart was all with the horse. Why had they united to torture the poor creature?

The rider had flung himself from the saddle barely in time, but, when he rose, he apparently refused to continue the contest. Yet still the struggles of the stallion were not over. A third rider presented himself, distinguished by a blue bandanna and a sombrero whose belt gleamed with pure, burnished gold. He mounted as the other had done. Once more the battle began, and this time it lasted thrice as long. Tom could see that the young stallion had grown black with sweat. But he fought on as though he were muscled with springs. In the end, a leap, a jarring landing, and a spring to the side unseated the rider.

He fell in a cloud of dust, while the tormented horse fled to the farther side of the corral and tried to leap to safety beyond the bars. He was roped and brought down heavily on his side, and, while he lay there, the dismounted man of the blue bandanna approached and quirted the helpless body brutally.

This, however, seemed too much for even the other savages. They drew the fellow away, the stallion was allowed to climb to his feet, and was led away, and the group dispersed.

But the heart of Tom followed the beautiful bay, for on the morrow, would not the torture begin again? And would they not persist until they had broken his spirit and his heart? Savagely he shook his fist at the backs of the disappearing men. Jerry, comprehending the anger, although not its cause, stopped in his digging for a ground squirrel and looked up with a growl among the trees.

But after that Tom turned eastward again, and Jerry went joyously in the lead. They had both had too much of men. A bright-running trout stream a mile away, however, was too great a temptation to them both. There they paused while Tom caught their supper. He risked a fire, carefully made of dead wood so that there would be as little smoke as possible, and broiled a small part of his catch for himself, while Jerry devoured the remainder.

When that meal was ended, the twilight was descending, and Tom, with a filled stomach, found that the vision of the bay still haunted him. It seemed to fill his mind, that picture of the horse. He began to remember an old mustang that his father had used for mountain work. Even that treacherous brute he had loved, for men are born to love horses or to despise them, and Tom was one of the former.

It seemed to him that, if he could have that magnificent creature in the mountains, his happiness would be complete. Not to ride, to be sure, for his own legs were good enough to carry him where he wished to go, and, when he was tired, there was the exhaustless Jerry, to carry him on.

But how could he take a wild horse from men who were armed with guns?

That question lay heavily on the mind of Tom as the twilight thickened. He sat broodingly beside the fire until Jerry began to growl, so great was his eagerness for the return journey to twice-traveled fields. But Tom shook his head. That very insistence confirmed him in his new desire.

"The point is," he said to the huge bear, "that I've got to have that horse. And if I can't have him, I've got to have one more look at him. Stay here, Jerry. I'm going back!"

It was a command that Jerry understood. He stood still with an almost human groan, and Tom turned, drew tight his belt, and started back at a run.

He never walked when he was bent on business. Walking was the gait for leisure and careful observation. But he had learned to read even a difficult trail while he ran, and now he jogged back through the trees, twisted aside into the head of the cañon to his right, and then let out a link and raced blithely across the rolling ground until he turned the point of the promontory and the ranch houses were in view.

The instant he saw the first lighted window, he slowed to a walk. He had learned from Jerry's mother a lesson of caution that he never forgot. Jerry himself was an alert hunter. He could not cross a clearing, no matter how small, without first pausing an instant to take in his surroundings. He seemed to carry in the back of his brain a chamber crowded with memories of dangers that had come upon his ancestors. He suspected every tree, apparently, lest it might turn into a monster.

There was something of the same manner in Tom as he approached the house. He took advantage of every tree. He skulked swiftly down the hollows. He crawled on hands and knees over the knolls. When he came to the first barn, his caution redoubled. Around it he stole. And then he heard men's voices—many of them. A shudder crept down his spine as he listened, for the memory of the stranger in his cave was still rank. And, never having matched his strength against another man, how could he know that even that giant of a man would have been helpless now against his own lightning speed of hand and foot and that strange strength with which his muscles had been seasoned by those years of exposure and constant exercise? All he knew was that he had been helpless in the hands of a man once before, and he felt that he would be helpless again.

Nevertheless, he went on. He came in view of the house

itself, long, low, thrown loosely together, with only three lighted windows in its length. These were open, and from one of them came the tumult of voices.

He stole to it and looked in. What he saw was a group of four men around a table, playing cards. Each man was flanked with a glass, and there were bottles behind the chairs from which, now and again, they poured a trickle of amber liquid into their glasses, drank, and played again. The talk came at intervals. Sometimes there was a solemn silence while the cards were sent flashing out around the table and the hands were picked up. Then they began to push out money toward the center of the table. Some of the cards were discarded. Others were drawn, and more money was stacked, all in a deadly seriousness. But Tom cast only an idle glance of wonder at their occupation. He gave his more serious attention to the faces of the players.

Chapter Seventeen

PETER IS TAKEN

If he had traveled around and around the country, he could not have found four more repulsive faces. Greed, ferocity, cruelty were ingrained in each. It was no practiced eye with which Tom looked upon them, but instinct taught him all he needed to know. How different they were from John Parks. The surety grew in him that his father had been a different breed of man, a single exception. But the rest of the human race was evil, all evil. He felt his detestation grow, for how could all of these be compared in worth with that beautiful horse he had seen them torturing that day?

Here the man of the blue bandanna pushed back his chair. His pile of money was gone. "I'm busted, boys," he said, "but who'll stake me twenty?"

"On what, Hank?" asked another. "What's your security?"

"On old Peter," said Hank.

"Twenty dollars on that hoss?" murmured the other.

"Well?" asked Hank aggressively.

"I'll tell you," said the other, "Peter is worth something in the thousands . . . or else he ain't worth a cent. And, speaking personal, I say he ain't worth a cent."

"Hey!" responded Bill. "He's got the looks. There ain't no doubt of that. But looks ain't what a gent can sit a saddle on. Matter of fact, the man ain't born that can ride Peter."

"That's fool talk!" cried Hank. "Why, anybody can lead Peter around."

"Who's talking about leading?" answered Bill. "What good does it do a gent to have a hoss that he can lead if he can't ride it? And nobody can ride Peter. Look at Sam Dunbar. Didn't he try his prettiest on Peter today? But after he got throwed, he had enough. He wouldn't go back at Peter."

"Dunbar's nerve is gone," said Hank sullenly.

"What about your nerve? Why didn't you tackle him after he threw you?"

Hank sat silently and glared. He was plainly hunting for words but could find no retort.

"You take my advice," said Bill. "Peter has a pile of looks, but that's all. All the good he'll do you will be to run up a feed bill. If I had him, I'd turn him into dog food *pronto*."

Hank sprung to his feet. "Boys," he said, "ain't there a one of you what would advance me something on Peter?"

They shook their heads.

"Yet you all wanted him bad enough when he was running loose. When he was running through the hills with that gang of mustangs, you all sure enough wanted Peter bad. Every man here rode for him. But, when I creased him and got him, you say he ain't worth nothing. Is that sense?"

"Talk for yourself, Hank," they told him. "We don't want him. All he'll do for a gent is to bust his neck. He's turning into a killer. That's the worst kind . . . them that are quiet as lambs till they feel a cinch bite into them. They ain't no use, ever. You got him rope broke easy, but you'll never break him for the saddle. If you want some money, put up your gun. I'll give you something for that!"

Hank sneered. "Give up my gat with Joe Saunders in town?" he said fiercely. "I ain't that much of a fool!"

"Then use your gat to turn Peter into dog meat, if you want," said Bill, "but don't hold up the game no longer. Your deal, Sam."

Hank regarded the others with a concentrated malevolence for a moment, but suddenly he jammed his hat upon his head, turned on his heel, and strode from the room.

"Wait a minute . . . ," began Bill.

"Shut up," said Sam. "If he wants to kill the hoss, let him do it before the hoss kills him. And that's what it would come to one of these days."

"But a hoss like Peter . . . ," began Hank.

"I know," said Sam. "A hoss like Peter looks like a picture, but that's all the good he is. He might as well stay on the page of a book. All the good in him is to make a pile of talk."

Tom recoiled from the window.

So that was to be the end of beautiful Peter—a bullet through the head and then the buzzards. He stole around the house just as the back door of it banged, and Hank stepped out into the night and walked straight for the corrals with the speed and the decision of a man bent on business. Like a moving shadow, Tom drifted behind him.

In the corral, Hank advanced with a rope, and Tom saw him go directly up to Peter. There was no mistaking the horse even in the darkness. That mobile and beautiful animal had a light of its own.

Tom wondered to see the great horse submit so calmly to the rope that was put around its head. Then Peter was led out from the corral and tethered to the fence. A gun gleamed in the hand of Hank.

"Now, damn your soul," growled Hank, "you've got out to the end of your rope, and you're going to be flopped. I've stood a whole lot from you. Take it by and large, I put in six months getting in a shot at you. And when that slug knocked you down without killing you, I sure thought I was going to make a pile of money out of you. I figured I had the fastest thing on four feet that was running through the mountains. But you ain't done me no good. You've got me busted. I'm through with you. Here's the end of your trail. I might turn you loose, but I ain't going to let it be said that I had six months' work for nothing."

The gun raised in a steady hand. Tom slipped closer. His heart was hammering at the top of his throat. He could barely breathe, so great was his fear. There was the knife, to be sure. But he could not strike it into a human body—from behind. Something in his heart made that impossible. Yet, if he grappled that man hand to hand, how could he match that matured strength of Hank?

Desperately he set his teeth. There was no time to reflect. He leaped from behind and caught Hank in his arms. To his amazement the body of Hank seemed to crumple to water. Strength? He knew at a touch that he could break the man in two! But the sense of power made him gentle. There was only a strangled gasp from Hank as the revolver was torn from his hand and he was laid upon the ground. Peter snorted and stepped back.

"Now listen," said Tom, while all his blood was in a riot from that easy victory. "Listen to me. If you try to call the others by yelling for them, I'll send a slug into you. That'll make one less to follow me. If you even try to stand up, I'll shoot. And you can be sure that I won't miss!"

There was not a word from Hank. His body merely stiffened. But in the meantime, the possession of that loaded gun meant a world of added power to Tom. He took off the heavy cartridge belt from his victim. He buckled it around his own hips. He dropped the revolver into the holster. Then he went to Peter. But there seemed to be no need for his soothing voice. The strength of a rope was a fact that the stallion had learned first of all from his contact with men, and, although he might be in terror for his life, he would not pull back against it. It had burned into his flesh too often before.

He stood patiently while Tom unknotted the rope. At the first tug of the rope against his neck, he stepped out to follow the new master. That act of obedience thrilled Tom with a sudden and strange gratitude, a wealth of tenderness. In his heart of hearts he vowed that Peter should never regret that step. He sent a last word to Hank.

"I'm still watching you!" he called softly, then broke into a jogging run. Peter came readily at his heels. Once around the edge of the corral, he increased the pace to his full speed, and still Peter followed without once drawing back on the rope. But, as Tom rounded the edge of the cliff from the top of which he had first had a view of the horse, he heard a sudden hubbub behind him, and voices shouting, carrying clearly through the mountain night. The alarm had been given, and in another moment the pursuit on horseback would begin!

Chapter Eighteen

FLIGHT FOR THE WOODS

The temptation was to strain forward still faster, but even the greyhound strength of those mountain-trained legs of Tom, even that almost exhaustless lung power, could not sustain a sprint for three miles, and it was fully that distance to the head of the cañon where the timber and the rough ground would help to slow up the pursuers. So Tom calculated the distance and diminished his gait, although it took all his willpower to enable him to do it.

As for the danger of capture, he knew nothing of the unwritten law that makes horse stealing equally culpable with murder in the West, but no tale could have terrified him more than he already was. Dread of death kept him running. Now and again he would leap into a sprint involuntarily.

Behind him came a distant whooping, and then the beating of many hoofs again was audible. He cast a glance behind him. There came Peter, the stallion, his ears pricking as though he rejoiced in the running—there came Peter, rocking along at a lazy canter. Oh, to be mounted on the back of that king of horses! Then how he would laugh at pursuit. It would be like adding wings. But far away over the starlit cañon floor, he could see the horsemen beginning to loom.

They swept close and closer at a terrific speed. Yet, measuring the distance to the woods ahead of him, he knew that he must save his strength. There was still an open mile between him and the woods, and even in the woods he must still be prepared to run on, for they would spur ahead as fast as they could, weaving through the trees.

That last mile was an untold agony, for a gun barked behind him. It was a random shot, but it made Tom leap ahead. His driving legs were numb to the knees, to the hips. His lungs were filled with fire. There was not enough air in the universe to give him one sweet, fresh breath.

How those wild riders behind him were gaining! He began to dread to glance back, so much more clearly were they growing upon his eyes. And now he threw caution to the winds, and he cast all his power into the last spurt. The woods grew up, black and tall. They were like a promise of heaven to Tom, with those increasingly loud hoof beats ringing in his ears. The pursuers, feeling that the race was close, opened with a rattling volley. But men cannot shoot straight from horseback, and the bullets flew wild, singing around Tom, while he raced on with head straining back, with mouth gaped wide, with eyes wild, with his long hair blown back from his shoulders.

He was lost, he told himself. He could hear the panting of their horses. Or was it the breathing of Peter, coming with such maddening ease behind him? Then suddenly his eyes cleared. The woods were only a step before him.

He leaped behind the first trunk. Peter swung into the shadow nearby. Tom jerked the revolver from the holster and fired blindly at the rushing forms. A yell of alarm answered him. The riders split to the right and the left, wheeled, and scurried away. He grew weak with relief and fired again—into the air. But it brought another volley of curses from the four riders.

They would circle back and steal into the woods to try to head him off. But that was a game at which they would find him hard to beat, unless he had lost his cunning in woodcraft. He started on again up the slope, with Peter dancing anxiously at his heels, sniffing and snorting at the strange shadows, then stealing along noiselessly as the spirit of the wilderness came heavily upon his heart with fear. The open hills, the wide plains were the domain of Peter, and, in this forest darkness, he was glad of company, even if that company had to be detested man.

In the meantime, the lungs of Tom had grown cool. His trembling knees regained their strength. Presently he was swinging along at a brisk gait, more himself every moment. He thought of Jerry. The ideal way would be to head straight for the upper mountains where horsemen could least easily follow. He should ride Jerry and lead the stallion. But he knew that the horse would be paralyzed with fear near the grizzly, for all things that lived and ran wild dreaded Jerry. How could he handle the two together?

Near the place where he had camped by the brook, he tethered Peter to a tree, and the horse cowered close to it, eying in terror the moving shades of the woods. Tom went on to the grizzly and found him rooting in the bank of the stream. He brought him back within view of the horse.

The effect on both was exactly what Tom had foreseen. Jerry heaved instantly on his hind legs and stood immense, growling. Poor Peter went back to the limit of his rope and there crouched like a great cat, overcome with nameless terror. If they were to become better acquainted, the night was not the time for it. Tom thought of another expedient. He loosed Peter from the tree and started on up the hillside briskly—for who could say when the pursuers would come upon his trail? He could not realize that the night that was such an open book to him was closed to ordinary men. Peter followed, knocking his fore hoofs against Tom's heels in his eagerness to get away from Jerry, and Jerry came grumbling and rumbling in the distance, a very bewildered and angered bear. Yonder went his human friend—master, he could hardly be called. With Tom wandered what was to Jerry simply an ample store of food going on foot. Yet when Jerry pressed close, there came from Tom the whistle that to the big bear meant danger ahead.

Half a dozen times he heard that whistle as he drew near. Each time he lifted to his hind legs as a wise bear should and sniffed the air for the scent of an enemy, but found no trace. Finally he understood that, while Tom accompanied the horse, he wished Jerry to stay in the background. A bear will sulk exactly as a human being sulks. So when Jerry perceived the desire of his friend, he promptly turned around and melted into the forest.

Tom paused and looked back after him in great anxiety. But after a moment he went on. He was wise enough to know that it was foolish to attempt to read the mind of the grizzly. That cunning fellow might have disappeared in order to trail them closely at hand, but secretly. Or perhaps Jerry would get ahead of them in order that he might watch from cover as they passed. That was exactly what happened, for, when he paused at daybreak upon the top of a mountain, he found Jerry on the upper side, although the big fellow instantly dropped his head and began to dig in the ground as if he had gone there for the sole purpose of finding delectable roots.

But now, since daylight was come, Tom tethered the horse to a sapling around which the grass grew, thick and long, and, while the stallion ate, he stood back and looked at his prize for the first time. What he saw was more than he could have hoped. To be sure, the horse was thin. Every rib along his side could be marked, and on his flanks were still the crimson signs of whip and spur. He had been most cruelly handled.

No wonder that he shrank from the lifted hand of Tom. No wonder that his great eyes blazed with terror when Tom came near.

Wild rage boiled up in the heart of the youth. For here was a creature intended by nature surely to be handled with affection alone, and they had tried to beat it into submission. He gloried with a sudden joy in the knowledge that at least men had failed to have their will of the horse. For his own part, how utterly contented he would be to have this king of the plains to watch, to talk to so that the sharp little ears would prick at the sound of his voice, to feed until he was sleek and round of barrel. Here was companionship. To be sure, if ever he could persuade the stallion to permit him to sit on its back—the heart of Tom jumped.

Then he sat down cross-legged on the grass and drew out from a pouch at his side the quantity of crushed, dry corn that he always carried when he traveled. He held out a quantity of it in both cupped hands. No matter that the stallion, not grown accustomed to the man-food given to horses, sniffed it and then backed away, his ears flattened against his neck. The patience of Tom was not that of the ordinary man. He had been taught in the school of the wilderness. He had learned the endless patience of Jerry, who would dig two hours for the sake of a single woodchuck. And if quiet and gentleness and unending endurance would win, Peter should be his horse in the end, body and soul.

Chapter Nineteen

SIX MORE YEARS PASS

"Of course," said Gloria, "if you have made up your mind to believe, no one can dissuade you."

"Don't be disagreeable, Glory," said her father with a frown.

"I'm trying my level best not to be," said Gloria, "but, ever since you hunted in Africa, you've been entranced by fables," and she smiled as her father bit his lip in vexation.

She was probably the only person in the world who refused to take her distinguished father altogether seriously. Others were mightily impressed by the reputation of this man who could shoot lions one day and write learnedly about them from a biological viewpoint on the next, and who, above all, had taken more folklore out of Africa than almost any other human being. But to Gloria, John Hampton Themis was first and foremost the father of Gloria. Besides, she had not wanted to take this trip into the mountains. At eighteen, Paris was infinitely more attractive. Although she had forced herself to be amiable when her father insisted that she learn something about her own country before she pried into "the truth about Europe", she could not help taking out some of the disappointment in such petty badgering as this.

As a matter of fact, she had found the valley of the Turnbull far more interesting than she had expected. In her blood ran some of her father's fiery love of saddle and rifle and the arduous hunting trails. At eighteen Gloria could walk down an average man when it came to mountain climbing, and she was a little proud of that fact. Yet Paris now and then swam back upon her ken, and, when it did, as at the present moment, she could not avoid being a little disagreeable.

Her father had always attempted to convince her by reason and not to overwhelm her by the force of parental authority. He sat down to reason now. "I simply wish to submit the facts to you, my dear," he said. "After you have examined them, you can make up your mind for yourself, Glory."

"Fire away," said Gloria, and she lighted a cigarette.

"You're smoking simply to irritate me," said John Hampton Themis.

"I'm smoking because it's modern," retorted Gloria.

"Modern be hanged," said Themis. "Such modernity is ruining American girlhood."

"That," said Gloria, "is a bit strong."

John Hampton Themis glared, then shrugged his shoulders, and sat back. But when a moment later Gloria laid aside the cigarette, he noted it with infinite satisfaction. As always, she only resisted to make her point, and then she yielded completely. She was more like a boy than a girl, he had decided.

"I told you yesterday," he said, "the story of the Indian and the man whose dogs were killed."

"I remember it all," she said. "The man heard his dogs raise a clamor as though they had scented a bear. But when he went out, he found two of the dogs stabbed to death and a third with a crushed skull as though a bear had struck it. And when they examined the trail the next morning, they found that a man's moccasined footprints were mixed with those of a huge grizzly. Isn't that right?"

"Yes."

"And the deduction is that a man had helped the bear to fight the dogs."

"Why not?"

"Why not? Well, isn't it absurd on the face of it? Besides, all this happened years ago. You know how a story can grow in six years . . . yes, or six days."

"Please be reasonable, Glory. There are three honest men who swear to the truth of that story."

"You think that this Indian had actually tamed a grizzly? A grizzly!"

"Why not? It has been done before. There's the story of Ben Adams. He trained one after another. They actually fought for him against their own kind."

"When did Ben Adams live?"

"Because a thing happened seventy years ago," cried her father, "does that turn it into a fable?"

"Usually," she answered calmly.

"*Hmm,*" he said. "You're in a bad humor today. But I'll convince you in spite of yourself that this is a trail worth running down. Let me tell you what I've learned in addition."

She shrugged her graceful shoulders.

"A day after the exploit of the dogs, a man named Hank Jeffries, a rough fellow who I've seen and talked with, went out to shoot an outlaw mustang, a stallion he had captured by creasing. It was a famous horse called Peter. But Peter, once captured, proved untamable. No one could sit the saddle on him for five consecutive minutes. Hank received several broken ribs and minor injuries from various attempts to ride the horse. Finally he invited three famous riders to his ranch. One by one they all tried the horse, and Peter won. So in the night Hank went out to shoot the creature. . . ."

"How terrible! Is that the sort of thing your precious Westerners, your romantic cowpunchers, will do? I'd rather shoot a man than a horse."

"So would a good many cowpunchers. But Hank is not exactly a citizen of the finest character. He has a black record. The killing of a horse wouldn't be the worst stain on his reputation, I understand. At any rate, he didn't kill Peter."

"Good!" cried Gloria.

Her father smiled at her enthusiasm. "No, when he raised the gun, a giant leaped on him from behind, took him with a terrific grip that crushed the wind out of him, threw him down to the ground, tore the gun out of his hand, and threatened to kill him if he stirred. Then the stranger took the lead rope of the horse and made off into the night . . . a huge man with long hair that flowed down almost to his shoulders. And he ran like the wind. He ran so fast, in fact, that, when Hank called his friends and they started in pursuit on their horses after only an instant . . . for the horses were saddled and waiting . . . they could not catch the stranger, although he had several miles to run."

"That," commented Gloria, "is plainly a fable. You must admit that it is."

"I went over the ground today," said the great hunter. "Even if they had had to capture their horses before they started, even if they had had to saddle them in the corrals, it would have required a great runner to get away from running horses into the shelter of the woods at the head of the cañon. Still, it's possible that a man of iron nerve and iron muscles, a natural runner of a race of runners, might have done that very thing. And it has to be admitted that this Indian did it. Four men wouldn't lie about such a point."

"They're sure he's an Indian?"

"Everything points to it . . . the moccasins in part, because, though a good many mountaineers use them, the average white man prefers boots. But most of all, his quiet ways and that long, flowing hair point to an Indian. No white man, accustomed to other men, could have gotten along for these six years without coming down to mix with society now and then. But this fellow has lived inside himself. It is really most remarkable!"

"But has he been seen at all during these six years?" asked the girl.

"Not actually seen, I believe," said the other thoughtfully. "But they know that he's around."

"And haven't they been able to run him down?"

"No. Several times he's come down from the mountains, however. The spring after the stealing of the mustang, a great bundle of beautiful beaver skins were brought down in the night and left at the house of Hank without word of who had brought them. It is generally taken for granted that the Indian brought them in payment for the horse that he had stolen. He has done the same thing at other times. Once the store was broken open in the town of Turnbull, yonder, and the next morning one rifle and a great stock of ammunition were found missing, but in return there was left a bundle of furs worth ten times the value of the stolen goods. On another occasion . . . you see that it must be the same man . . . a rancher's house was invaded, and a hundred pounds of ham and bacon were taken, along with other food and more ammunition. But again furs were left in payment."

"Oh," cried Gloria, "Dad, what a wonderful fellow that hermit must be!"

"The Indian, you mean," said Themis.

"Oh, well, call him that if you choose. But I for one don't think that an Indian has such a conscience. But how does he manage to steal so many things without being caught?"

"He has the courage of a fiend," said Themis. "He seems to laugh at the possibility of discovery. There are some uneducated people in the valley who are beginning to have a superstition that the Indian can actually go invisible. Of course, such rumors are bound to spring into the back of people's heads. You see, this cunning devil comes always at night. He seems to be able almost to see in the dark. He will enter a house from the rear while the inhabitants are in the front of it. He moves as silently as a shadow in his moccasins. He takes what he wants, and then he goes. From what I can gather, he has committed his robberies about twenty times during the past six years, and not once has a soul, besides Hank, had a glimpse of him."

"Not a single person?" said Gloria.

"Oh, there is a poor, half-witted fellow, a prospector, or one who calls himself a prospector," said Themis. "He has a wild tale, but, if I were to repeat it, you'd be convinced that the whole thing is simply a legend."

"On my honor," said Gloria, "I'm already a convert. I'd give my eyeteeth to see this Indian, or whatever he is."

"I'll tell you the yarn, then, though unquestionably there is more whiskey than truth in it. He declares that one moonlight night, in the mountains, he had made his camp in a hollow, and his blankets were put down behind a big boulder. He wakened at midnight with a great moon in the center of a clear sky, and, when he sat up, he saw . . . don't laugh, Gloria . . . he saw, he says, an immense grizzly bear, twice the size of any he had ever seen, coming down the mountainside with a tall, long-haired Indian sitting on its back, and behind them came a magnificent bay stallion, the most glorious horse he had ever laid eyes on, walking along of his free will, without a lead rope attached, but saddled, and with a pack behind the saddle. The idea was, you see, that the mountain was so steep that the Indian had gotten on the back of the bear to make it easier for his horse. A stiff wind was blowing from them to the prospector, so that the bear did not scent him.

"That strange caravan went by in silence. In utter silence, this poor half-wit declares. The very hoofs of the horse did not make a sound on the rocks. But, of course, I don't advance this yarn seriously. The idea of a man riding a bear is too preposterous. And the idea that a high-strung horse would come so near to a grizzly is even more absurd. But I don't need to say that some of these simple mountaineers declare that the story must be the truth."

"And I," said Gloria hotly, "am sure that it is the truth! Oh, how I should love to see him!"

"Now," said Themis, "I see that I've touched the romantic vein."

"You may laugh if you please," said the girl, "but, when you go on the trail after him, I'm certainly going to ride with you."

"You?" cried her father. "Absurd!"

"Not at all."

"But, my dear, this fellow is dangerous."

"But he's an honest man, Dad. He pays for all he takes."

"You can't take things and then pay for them as you please," said her father. "Ask the man whose dogs were killed, what he would do if he could get a chance to send a bullet into this Indian. Ask Hank, for instance, what he would do. And, above all, ask the poor sheriff, whose life has been hounded because he can't make the capture. The man who held office when the Indian began these excursions into Turnbull valley was fairly laughed out of office. The second man stood the gaff his whole four years, and, when he ran again, he received exactly twelve votes. The poor devil that has the job now is more to be pitied than despised. Everyone of those sheriffs has been a capable man, but they can't follow a fellow who seems to be able to make his trail disappear at will."

"Yes, but what of the trails of the horse and the bear?"

"People around here declare that he can make the trails of all three disappear like magic when he pleases. I suppose a hundred hunting parties have gone out to get him, equipped with dogs and fine horses and men who are expert riflemen. But they have always failed. Think of it! They have failed so miserably that they haven't laid eyes on the Indian either by night or day, save for Hank and one half-wit, if he may be believed."

"Well," said Gloria, "everything that you say convinces me more and more. I'm going to ride with you when you hunt him. I only hope one thing . . . that you won't hunt to kill."

"Tush," said her father, shrugging his shoulders, "when a man defies society, he has to take the consequences. But this time I'm going to run him down. It won't be a matter of a day or two, or even a week or two, of running. I'm going to stay after this mystery until I have run it to the ground if it takes me all the summer. I have the best dogs, the best horses, the best guides that money can hire, and I have employed them all indefinitely."

"Then," said Gloria, "it is plain that you could take me along. I won't be a burden."

"Stuff!" said Themis. "I wouldn't dream of it."

But, nevertheless, he stared at his daughter with a species of dread. He foresaw trouble ahead.

Chapter Twenty

THEMIS'S PARTY

Only a rich man could have provided for such a summer. Only a genius could have selected so skillfully those who were to ride with him. In the entire range of the mountains, Themis could not have found five men better fitted to follow a long trail, an arduous trail, a trail that might come to a dangerous ending. In the first place, he made sure that every man was known for hardihood and skill as a mountaineer, familiar with the Turnbull valley and all the mountains of the region surrounding the valley, an expert trailer, and, above all, capable of using rifle or revolver with deadly effect. Not only that, but he made sure that all his men had shot before at human targets. There hardly existed unhung a blacker crew of rascals than the five he weeded out of many applicants—for the wages were large and the food would be good, and, given those conditions to prevail, he could pick who he would.

Every man of the five had a record, although some of them had not been in a penitentiary. There was Si Bartlett, a little, smiling, inoffensive man very fond of talk, with great, mild, brown eyes. Of his forty-five years no less than fifteen had been spent in prison in two terms, both for manslaughter; in each instance he had been pardoned before his term was up for the simple reason that no warden could believe that a man with such a face, such a voice, such a pair of eyes, such gentle manners, could be a murderer except by accident. But those who knew declared him to be a matchless and malignant fighter, one of those who love danger for its own sake, and bloodshed for the same reason. Yet he was appointed second in command by Themis. Character had nothing to do with his selections. Results were what he wanted.

Next came Red Norton, save that Red could hardly be put second to any man. He, also, had felt the shadow of a prison close over him. But with nine lives, men freely declared outside of courtrooms, he could not have paid for all his victims. He was a contrast to Si Bartlett, although just as dangerous. What made him less terrible was that his appearance advertised his true nature in advance. His huge body, the rank growth of red hair, which bristled on his face and head, his bold, staring blue eyes, his blunt manner—all announced the professional warrior.

The third of that noble crew was Dick Walker. Dick was the boy of the party. He was apparently just a big, laughing, good-natured child of twenty. But, when the pinch came, Dick was cold as ice and cutting as a steel edge. Older men who were apt to know predicted a long career and a black one for Dick. He had not seen the inside of a prison for the simple reason that no jury could pronounce a man with such a face and such ability to laugh guilty of murder. For the rest, he was a genius on the trail, as all men admitted, and he possessed an uncanny dexterity of hand that made him equally at home with a cowpuncher's rope or a cowpuncher's gun.

Dude Wesson was the cook. His nickname described him. He was a tall, lean man, with a starved face. His apparel ever showed signs of consummate care. Polish was never missing from his kit, and his boots were shined morning and even at noon to the amazement of those who did not know him. He was none of those who allow the face to become covered with a bristle of hairs that is shaved only every third day. It was said that he would rather have water for shaving than for drinking, even on a desert. His clothes, also, were never allowed to fall into disrepair, and a spot upon the trousers meant half an hour's work to this fastidious gentleman.

Naturally such a man was self-indulgent in the matter of food. His fleshless face belied an appetite that was omnivorous. He began early at the table, he ate with terrible velocity, and he kept at it long after the others were through. Yet, no signs of that voracious gourmandizing appeared in his starved body. No one could cook to suit him. Therefore, he cooked for himself and for the rest. He was self-appointed to the task, and he was forgiven his other faults for the sake of his skill over a campfire and his genius with venison and coffee. Those faults were taciturnity, a temper as uneasy as a hair trigger, and a sullen dislike of everyone. He, too, had escaped the prison for the reason that he always forced the other man to make the first move, trusting to his superior speed of hand, his superior steadiness in aiming, to kill his victim at the last instant. In all his fights he had accumulated not a scar. Such was Dude Wesson.

The fifth and last of the party was no other than Hank Jeffries. He was the least famous of the lot, but he was taken along partly because he knew the mountains better than the student knows his book, and partly because he was inspired by a prodigious hatred for the Indian. He had never forgiven the theft of the stallion. It mattered not that he had been on the verge of killing the animal. It was only more of a rankling wound in his malevolent soul that another should have been able to use that which he himself had not been able to master. Day and night, he dreamed of the battle that must at last take place between himself and the Indian.

To that end, he kept himself in constant fettle. He had begun a soberer life, because he did not wish to be taken unawares if the opportunity came. Day by day he practiced with his guns to make sure that he could make the best of the first opening. He had invested the last money he could borrow on his ruined ranch to buy two fast horses that should be ready for the pursuit. When he learned of the purpose for which John Hampton Themis was organizing the posse, he had come to the great man and begged with tears in his eyes to be granted the privilege of accompanying the party. At least, he could make himself useful on account of his skill in the handling of dogs.

Themis took him for the last reason as well as the others that have been mentioned. Even if Jeffries was not cast according to the heroic mold of the others, he was a man of talent, and the party could not get on without his skill. He had "learned" dogs in his childhood, and he had never forgotten the lessons. Not that he particularly loved them, but he knew their ways, and he could handle them in the field.

This was the more important to Themis because not the least important part of his posse consisted of the dogs. He had even sent to a distance and waited a week to secure a set of bloodhounds, and four of these long, low-geared, soft-eyed beasts were finally brought to him. Their noses were to be the first agency through which the trail would be unwound and the riddle solved.

But they were not the major portion of the dog pack. In addition, there were half a dozen mongrels of all sizes, shapes, and colors, but all valuable dogs on a bear trail where intelligence is needed. And it is an old tale that the nameless cur is the one with the peerless set of brains. Furthermore, the dog pack had its fighting, swift-running portion, consisting of eight big hounds with a strong strain of greyhound mixed with heavier and more powerful breeds. Two of them could pull down a timber wolf, for they were trained to fighting tactics. Four of them could worry a bear to death if they caught it in open country, and the eight could destroy any animal that walked if given a fair opportunity. Their noses were not altogether trustworthy, but, when the trail was hot, they could follow it well enough, and, the moment they had sight of the quarry and could get their heads up, they were off like eight streaks of murder bent on business.

There was another purpose for which those dogs could be used. While the bloodhounds were dawdling along the trail, untangling it slowly, but with the surety of death, these swift hounds would kill enough food for the entire pack. So long as there were rabbits in the mountains through which they trailed, there would be no need of worrying about the food of the pack.

Such was the outfit with which Themis stood prepared to start on his journey. As for horses, there were two of the finest sort for each man. Hank Jeffries had his own mounts, and each of the other four had a fast horse. Their auxiliary mounts alone had to be furnished by Themis, and he bought them regardless of expense. Altogether, he had invested a pretty penny in that expedition before the news came that started it on the trail.

That news came suddenly by night. Into the very town of Turnbull itself the marauder had come, opened the store, and taken out a new and fine saddle. On this occasion, he left no payment of furs. It might be that he had run short in his supply. It might be that he had decided that it was nonsense to pay for what he would take without making an exchange. The probability was that, before the year was out, he would bring down something in payment. The storekeeper was willing to wait. He had already done profitable business with this strangely generous being. But the community was not willing to wait. These dips out of the mountains by the

Indian, so often repeated, had made the town a laughing-stock. The next morning three distinct parties started on the trail.

The sheriff and his posse made up one. There was another, consisting of independent, irate citizens who had nothing better to do. The third party was that of Themis himself. On the floor of the store was found a crudely made pair of moccasins that had been discarded in favor of a shop-made brand. Those discarded moccasins were given to the dogs to establish the scent, and straightway the bloodhounds raised their mellow call and started away. They wound around behind the village where the prints showed that the marauder had walked leisurely. They came to the open, where he had begun to run with an amazingly long and regular stride. From that point he had darted across to the hills behind the Jeffries place. In the trees they found the spot where he had left his horse. Through the steep hills the three parties worked in unison, these grim and silent men. But presently the fugitive had descended into the more open and rolling country and had fled north.

On that section of the trail the better horses of the Themis party quickly told the tale of their worth. All day they raced north, and long before nightfall, as the trail veered sharply to the left and entered the mountains again, the sheriff's posse and the group of townsmen were left far out of sight to the rear.

Chapter Twenty-One

FIRST CAMP

At the first steep hillside they noticed a peculiarity. The man had dismounted from the horse and had struggled up the ascent on foot. Among those ragged rocks, he had evidently figured that he could climb far better than his horse, and he took the burden of his weight out of the saddle. Themis gave his order instantly, and his men came grumbling out of the saddle. They were fellows who lived in the stirrups, every one of them. But, when they had struggled to the top of the incline, they appreciated the value of that order, for their horses were in good condition, not half so winded as if they had been under the pull of the reins with a weight in the saddle during the labor.

It was a comparatively freshened lot of horses that now took up the journey across a rough, broken, upper plateau. But here another trail joined that of the horse. Hitherto, the bloodhounds had run steadily in the lead. But now the entire pack surged into the lead and left the bloodhounds far behind.

"Bear!" cried Hank Jeffries. "They've picked up a bear trail."

Sure enough, as they crossed a damp place near a natural spring that welled out of the ground, they saw the huge prints of a grizzly, the largest prints that Themis had ever seen. His heart leaped. All the story rushed back upon his brain, and here was the proof of it. Horse tracks and bear tracks went

133

side-by-side. But now the twilight was beginning, and he ordered a halt. It might well be that with a single drive tomorrow they could run down the fugitive, but for that purpose it was far better that they should be rested, man and beast. So they camped beside a brook.

Hank Jeffries took the hounds, hardly touched with fatigue by the day's work, to run down what he could in the hills nearby. For the rest of the men, Dude Wesson took command and began giving orders sharply as soon as their horses had been hobbled and turned out to graze. With brief, sharp words he ordered one to arrange stones for the fire, he commissioned two to cut wood, and another was directed to help with the preparation of the food. All obeyed without a murmur, for who does not stand in terror of the cook?

Themis himself made a point of taking up his share of the work, although it was long since he had spent such a day in the saddle, and he was thoroughly fagged. In a few moments, the fire was blazing, and food began to steam. Suddenly Dude Wesson straightened beside the fire and pointed a stiff arm down the slope, then turned to his work again without a word. Themis, looking in the designated direction, saw Gloria come riding toward them.

He was mute with wonder and anger. On she came! Where the upward pitch began, she dismounted, just as he had made his men dismount. Up the slope she climbed as briskly as any youth could have done. On the edge of the plateau she mounted and came to them at a swinging canter. She dismounted at a little distance, unstrapped a pack behind her saddle, and unsaddled and hobbled her horse and turned it to graze with the rest. Then she came in, carrying the pack slung over her shoulder, the heavy saddle on the other arm.

"Glory!" cried her father, finding his tongue at last. "What on earth has come into your head? Have you gone mad?"

"Never used better headwork," said Gloria mildly. "If I'd started out with you from town, you'd have sent me back by force, so I simply trailed you at a distance. It was very easy and perfectly safe. Not one of your entire gang looked behind during the trip. If the Indian had wanted to, he could have come in behind you and traveled along in perfect safety. I was in plain view twenty times. And now that I'm this far away from civilization, Dad, you certainly can't send me back through mountains infested with wild men."

Themis groaned as the truth of what she had said came home to him.

"Glory," he said bitterly, "I've spoiled you all your life. And this is the reward of my labor. But . . . don't you see? I hired these fellows for a man trail. Do you think they can be bothered taking care of a woman in the midst of their other work?"

She jerked up her chin. "Have I asked to be cared for?" she said hotly. "Not by any means. I've made up my own pack. I haven't taken a thousand pounds of tinned stuff along, as you've done, to kill your horses. I've cut myself down to essentials. I have a rifle and matches and salt and flour. I'll kill my own meat." As she spoke, she threw down a newly killed and cleaned rabbit. "I'll make my own living and I'll carry my own burdens. And if Mary Anne can't hold up her end with my weight on her back, I'll walk home." She turned and whistled to Mary Anne. The dainty-footed chestnut tossed up her head and whinnied a soft response.

"Heaven help me!" and Themis sighed. "The man was never born who could talk you down."

"Besides," said Gloria suddenly, "I don't think the men are so disgusted with me. Are you, Mister Wesson?"

The unexpected appellation of "Mister" was a shock to Dude Wesson. He looked up with a scowl from his cookery.

135

He found Gloria walking straight toward him. He got up and removed his hat—to rub his head. Suddenly the scowl melted from his face. A smile trembled like a frightened stranger on his lips, and he nodded.

"I guess you ain't going to be much in the way," said Dude graciously, and returned to his work, with a slightly heightened color.

John Hampton Themis simply filled his pipe and sat down to think and to watch. He had become a great deal of a philosopher since Gloria reached young womanhood. He had even referred to her as a "boiled-down education, hard to swallow but good for the insides." He thought of that now as he watched her go down the slope to join the wood gatherers. There she wasted no time in greetings but picked up a discarded axe and presently was swinging it with a fine and supple strength. Even the abysmal brute, Red Norton, paused to observe her workmanship. He found no fault with her. She was like Si Bartlett. She made up in skill what she lacked in power of body. She could send the axe home within a hair's-breadth of her aim. Red grunted with approval. In fact, in sheer hand magic, there was only one member of the party who excelled her, and that was the smiling and amiable young man-killer, Dick Walker.

A new thought came to Themis as he watched. She might be the influence that would keep the whole party cheerful on the trail, and men who laugh at their work can work three times as well as in a gloom of serious endeavor. Laughter clears the brain. For the rest, she would be as safe among these chosen villains as among men of her own kin.

She insisted on making her own campfire and cooking her own food, and she roasted her single portion and ate it before the others were half finished. Then she came over to join their circle.

136

It was a most formal crowd. Every man there had been accustomed to lord it over his fellows in whatever society he found himself, but here were four with equally sinister reputations, and a fifth not far behind them.

"If it ain't too much trouble," terrible Red Norton would say, "I'll have to be bothering you for that salt, Dick."

"Here you are," Dick would answer. "Just watch your plate, will you, Si? I'm going to get up, and I don't want no dust to be blowing into your chuck."

They would forget some of this formality later on, but, in the meantime, it was stilted conversation until Gloria threw in a bomb by asking how long they thought it would be before the Indian was run down. Straightway, each man raised his head with a grim smile. There was not one of the crew who did not feel that he could run any human being to the ground. But, now that five formidable trailers were assembled on fast horses, to say nothing of Themis himself, and with the assistance of that pack of dogs, they regarded their outfit as an irresistible juggernaut. They said so freely, each handing the praise deftly to the others.

"If a gent was to ask me," said Hank Jeffries, "how long it would take gents like Dude Wesson and Dick Walker to run down their man, I'd say it would be pretty *pronto*. But when you got Red Norton throwed in, and, when you got Si Bartlett on top of all them, I say that that Indian ain't going to keep a whole skin more'n tomorrow about sunset time."

But Gloria shrugged her shoulders. "I can't help thinking," she said, "if I could follow you so easily, why can't the Indian get away from you just as easily?"

It was a disagreeable and new phase of the subject, and it was promptly abandoned for more cheerful viewpoints. Half an hour later, the whole party was rolled in blankets.

For every member of the hungry crew, the night passed

like a second. Suddenly they heard the deep, bass voice of Dude Wesson grumble: "Turn out, everybody. It's pretty near sunup. Is this a picnic, maybe? Are we going to get started about noon? Hook onto an axe, a couple of you, and gimme some wood. I can't cook with air. Bartlett, are you too proud to peel potatoes? This ain't a hunting party, it's a rest camp!"

Those sullen exhortations began the day with a rush. Gloria saddled Mary Anne and cantered over the crest of the hill to a stream on the farther side. There she made her toilet and gave the men freedom to start the day with the customary groans and curses. By the time she came back, all was cheerful bustle, and the breakfast fire was blazing bright. The east was red with sunrise. The upper mountains were gleaming with light. Paris, for the first time since she left New York, was banished from the mind of Gloria.

Chapter Twenty-Two

PATIENCE SORELY TRIED

There followed three hours of serious labor through the mountains, and then the bloodhounds came to the bank of a creek and were silenced to the failure of the scent. They ran whining here and there. One of them swam across to the farther bank, but even there the trail could not be gained.

"He knows we're after him," said Hank Jeffries briefly. "Here's where the fun begins."

"No trouble at all!" called Themis cheerily. "He might cover his own trail, but he can't cover the trail of his horse and a grizzly bear. Impossible! Take the bloodhounds across. You send a pair of them upstream, and I'll take another pair down, and we'll pick up the trail directly."

It was done, but no trail developed. They had been a mile upstream and a mile down it, and there was no result. Hank Jeffries shook his head, cursing softly. The others were equally amazed.

"But, Dad," cried Gloria, "he can't have made the trails disappear into thin air!"

"Don't talk, please," snapped her father. "We have work to do. We'll try this bank of the creek, Hank."

So up the nearer bank of the creek they worked the hounds until, as on the farther side, they were stopped by waterfalls where the fugitives could not have gone. They reassembled at the starting place, the point where horse and bear had entered the water.

"In the meantime," groaned Themis, "the Indian has all this time gained. We'll never run him down today. Bartlett, what do you suggest?"

He shook his head. It was Dick Walker who offered the only possible advice.

"He's taken some way out of the water where he wouldn't leave a trail," he said. "Put out the dogs on each side of the creek a hundred yards away from it and see what you strike."

That was done, and half an hour later one of the hounds raised the familiar wolf wail and headed back into the mountains at a place 500 yards up the stream. The Indian had doubled back into the higher ground. All the party scurried to the spot. There were the trails leading out of a clump of bushes. Now that the scent was located, the track of the hunted man was instantly evident. He had gone up the creek to a broad, flat-topped rock that was close to the shore. From this he had made a long leap, clearing the bank of the creek and landing seven or eight feet away in the center of a clump of shrubbery, the outer part of which still stood up and revealed no break. From that place he had jumped into a similar clump, and so to another, until he cleared a considerable distance from the water. Then he had struck out. He had called the horse and the bear, and these animals, marvelously trained, must have followed in his exact footsteps. Here he had mounted again, and the trail went off up the slope.

But a half hour had been wasted in picking up the broken trail, and in that time the pursued man, even if he chose to go leisurely, could have placed five miles of mountain going between himself and the hunters. It was plain that only the greatest good luck could bring them up with the fugitive that day. But they struck out resolutely. All of them were too seasoned to the trail to be greatly cast down by a single disappointment, and, although Gloria felt at once that the task was hopeless, she could not but admire the way the rest of them went ahead.

"The point is," said her father, falling back beside her, "that this is a campaign, not a pursuit. And we're going to stick to the campaigning until we've cornered him."

They dipped over the next ridge and into a valley. Rather, it was a gorge, sloping easily down the side from which they had come, but cut to a cliff on the opposite wall. The hounds were heading up the valley along this wall when there came a sharp spat of a bullet on a rock before them, and, as they recoiled, half a dozen shots followed, crowding them back, although all went scatheless. Their mellow voices fell away to sharp squeals of terror overcome by the sounds of the reports of the rifle as these came lagging behind the swift bullets. For a moment the air was thick with the echoes of the gun, the voices of the dogs, and the angry and astonished shouts of the men as they scattered for cover behind the boulders.

There they cowered, anxiously searching the top of the cliff for the marksman. No sign of him was there. Five or ten minutes of worry followed. Suddenly Gloria stood up from behind her rock.

"Don't you see?" she explained. "He isn't shooting to kill. It was beautiful marksmanship. But he sent the bullets just ahead of the dogs each time. He didn't want to kill even the dogs, and it stands to reason that he wouldn't touch human beings. He simply wanted to show us that we were at his mercy."

The posse came out, one by one, and resumed their places in the saddle in a sullen silence. Plainly Gloria was right. Having run into such an ambush, they were ashamed to continue the trail after being at the mercy of their enemy. But the shame wore off and was succeeded by hot anger. He had been playing with them, declared Red Norton, pushing his horse into the lead at the heels of the bloodhounds. And he, Red Norton, would go ahead and prove that no man in the universe could make a fool of him once without living to be sorry for it.

The others declared that this was the right attitude and they went on more vigorously than ever through the rough country, pushing the dogs with an ever increasing energy. Gloria took the first opportunity to have a serious talk with her father.

"For my part," she said, "I think the best thing would be to let him go his way. For one thing, he has a sense of humor. Imagine him lying up there among the rocks and laughing when we heard his bullets and tumbled off our horses to get behind the rocks. A man who has a sense of humor can't be really bad."

"He has an educated sense of humor, then," said Themis, who was irritated in soul and body by a badly sun-scorched neck. "He has a sense of humor that makes me want to force him to laugh on the other side of his face."

"I admit"—and Gloria chuckled—"that you weren't exactly an heroic figure when you tumbled in behind that boulder."

"Confound it, Glory," he protested, "you'll never forget that! If I ever talk of hunting between this and my death day, you'll trot out the story of how I ran for cover. This bit of work had been laid out, and it has to be competed."

"But he has made fools of all of us," said Gloria.

"He has had luck," admitted her father grudgingly, "but it's nonsense to think that one man, no matter how well he may know these mountains, can dodge such a crew as I have brought together . . . at least for any length of time."

"And when he's cornered, what crime will he be tried for?"

"Horse stealing."

"A horse he paid for?"

"Ask Hank Jeffries if he agreed to take any payment. No, my dear, a man can't go ahead taking what he pleases and paying what he pleases. And how will he account to the man whose dogs he killed?"

"But I say," said Gloria, summing up in a woman's fashion, "that he's done nothing wrong. I pity him."

Themis did not care to argue. Two hours later, they ran into another trail problem that had been neatly constructed around a creek, and, even though they had already had a symptom of the tactics of the fugitive, it took another hour to unravel the difficulty.

Yet they struck into the trail again through the late afternoon, and, when they camped at sunset, it was a disgruntled, weary party. Gloria, however, had enjoyed the day thoroughly, for she rode carelessly along, with no thought of the fugitive in her brain, with no desire to overtake him. Her mind was simply filled with the beauty of the mountains through which they were traveling. Those rough-headed peaks against the tender blue of the sky, those thickly forested little valleys, with the white crash of a waterfall streaking the mountainside, and the pure sapphire of a still lake below— these were the things that filled up her eyes so that sometimes she broke into song. As they climbed closer to the huge, naked region above timberline, with a colder and a purer air, and with the horses laboring more heavily, her spirits rose.

To be happy is a wearying thing. When she fell asleep that night, it was to fall into a profound slumber. Yet even that slumber was stirred with dreams, and they were dreams of the purest delight—of walking through meadows where strange and delicately scented flowers bloomed, flowers whose names she could not tell—of listening to the liquid voices of streams—of breathing an air that was an intoxication of enjoyment.

She wakened to find that one part of her dream lingered into the daylight to a truth. Yonder was the tall form of Dude Wesson booming out his call to rise for the work of the day. But her blanket and the ground around her head were covered with flowers from the summits—forget-me-nots and daisies and goldenrod and silver and blue columbine and other flowers of delicate colorings and exquisite fragrances that were new to her. She swept up an armful of them. They were already slightly withered where they had laid on the dry blanket, but where they had been placed on the ground about her head there was first a layer of damp moss so that they might be preserved. She gazed in wonder and delight.

Which of the men could have done this thing? Which of the strange and apparently hard-hearted fellows could have been capable of that dainty tribute? Which of them, apparently all fast asleep before she closed her eyes, could have risen and worked for an hour or even more to collect these prizes? For there was no sign of a blossom near the camp.

There was only one possibility—Dick Walker. But, even as her glance fastened upon Dick, she saw him tilting a flask to his lips. He was taking his regular morning bracer before he could gain the strength to open his eyes and begin the day's work. No, such a man as Walker could not have done it.

But who else was there? The sunburned neck and the hard ride certainly removed her father from the list of possibilities, even if he could ever have been suspected. She sat amazed while the deep voice of the cook suddenly thundered: "Those dogs, Jeffries . . . you got to watch 'em, or I quit as a cook. They've swiped a whole side of bacon . . . or pretty near a whole side!"

That announcement brought the other men in a cluster about him. Furiously he pointed out where the meat was taken.

"But look here, Wesson," said Themis at last, "is it like a hungry pack of dogs to steal one piece of meat out of a hamper and leave another behind? Do dogs ordinarily close a cover they had lifted?"

All stood aghast. The girl drew the flowers closer, breathless with a wild surmise.

"A man stole it? But what use would any of us have for bacon?" began Si Bartlett. Suddenly he cried in a shrill voice: "Good Lord, you don't mean to say that the Indian came right down to our camp last night? That he was here among us?"

"However," said Themis, "we'll find out. Start the hounds, Hank."

Jeffries loosed the bloodhounds. They nosed the old trail carelessly, circled away, and suddenly struck a fresh one that darted straight up a steep slope covered with shrubs.

"By the gods!" roared Red Norton, who had gone to explore. "Here's where the hound came, and looked us over, right behind the boulder near where Miss Themis was sleeping. And . . . how come all these flowers?"

"I found them all around me when I woke up," said the girl. "And . . . oh, Dad, what a strange and beautiful thing it was for him to do."

"Strange and beautiful nonsense!" exclaimed her father. "Indian foolishness is what I'd call it. But, good heavens, how did he get into camp among all these dogs? Did he turn himself into a ghost?"

One by one, the men came and took up the flowers. Hank Jeffries was away whistling in the hounds.

"When I get him," said Dick Walker softly, "I'll take

these flowers out of his back."

He darted at the girl a keen side glance—no more. Yet it was eloquent of the truth that poor Dick was a victim where many another man had fallen before him, and where many a one would fall in the time to come. Gloria saw and knew and understood. What girl, innocent as she may be, does not? She was more interested, however, in the black frown that had overclouded the brow of her father. He stared at her with a sort of terror.

"Now," he said, "I'll stay by this trail if it leads down to Hades. This nonsense has to be stopped. After this we'll keep a watch around our camp."

But the others said nothing at all. Breakfast was eaten in silence, for this last trick had been too much for the hardiest of them. They had been made fools of the day before. But to have their camp visited in the middle of the night, to have food stolen from under their noses, to have a sort of silent flirtation started with a girl who was under their protection, and all this by the very man whose life they were hunting—that, indeed, was too much.

Chapter Twenty-Three

THE BREAKING POINT

Compared to this third day, the work of the preceding days was a mere nothing. In the first place, the trail led straight to a cliff, or what was almost a sheer rise of rock. The dogs could make it easily enough, and so could the men, but it was folly to attempt to get the horses up that murderous ascent. Yet up that very place Peter had been brought. Themis and Si Bartlett climbed far enough up the rocks to make sure. They saw the marks that the hoofs of the big horse had made as, with a daring and nimbleness unaccountable in a horse, he had worked to the top. He had made use of ledges and small footholds, which even a mountain sheep might have considered twice before using.

There was nothing for it but to marvel at the prowess of Peter and to take their own horses around a four-mile trail in order to come to the top of the summit. There, to their consummate fury, they found that the daring fugitive had waited until they were well committed to the roundabout way, and then he had traveled down the edge of the cliff and taken another and easier course to the ground. Even so, it was incredible that a horse should have made the descent. It had been done at considerable risk. Thrice they saw marks that proved that he had slid into the danger of death in getting down to the bottom of the gorge beneath. But down he had gone, while the saddle and the pack, perhaps—since nothing seemed impossible to this miraculous trainer of wild beasts—

had been carried by the grizzly.

But, no matter how the riddle was explained, it remained necessary for them to retrace their steps and to take the roundabout way down to the level going once more. Two precious hours had been consumed by the climb and the descent and the unraveling of that trail problem before the bloodhounds struck onto the trail again.

But now they followed it with utter indifference. Indeed, ever since the morning they had done their work as though weary of it, and, as for the mongrels and the big, fighting hounds, they lagged in the rear or coursed rabbits and would not pay the slightest attention to the work in hand.

Hank Jeffries had the only possible explanation. He declared that when the Indian came into camp the preceding night, he had managed to make friends with the entire pack. That explained the silence in which they had permitted him to come and go. That explained their negligence on the trail.

"Because," said Hank, "a dog is like any other critter. It works a pile better when it figures that it's after something it would like to chew or tree. But these dogs, they ain't got no interest in the Indian. They've seen him, they've nosed him, and they've been patted by him, most like. Maybe he brought in something for them to eat. I dunno how he done it. The Lord only knows. I'd've figured that Simpkins dog to chew up any man that tried to come near him. Look at me. I been with him 'most a week, now, but I can't put a hand on him. He's a regular killer. We ain't handling ordinary things with this Indian. He's got a sort of bad medicine. But I'll do the best I can to get the hounds worked up to the trail."

He lived up to his word. He was indefatigable in his efforts. But he could not make them run a hundred feet ahead of him on the trail before their heads would come up and they would start idling and playing with one another, and looking back to their master as though they wondered what on earth was the purpose in continuing on that course.

Such trailing meant slow work. By noon they had traveled hardly ten miles from their starting point. Si Bartlett summed up the result of their combined efforts: "We ain't done enough to keep that Peter hoss warm."

In the afternoon they tried to rush the trail, relying simply upon their ability as trailers by the eye, but after an hour they gave up the effort. Before that time was ended they struck a neat problem in the midst of some granite and shrubs, a tangle of which they could not make a head until the dogs had been persuaded to unravel it.

Just as they were heading along at a brisk gait for the first time in the day, they struck another murderous slope. This time they managed to go up it, but it was slow, slow work, and they had to take a horse at a time, which meant two trips for the entire party. They found themselves in a sort of badlands at the top of the rise. Worst of all, the night was coming on, horse and man were weary, and there was no water.

Bartlett and Jeffries made a short excursion on two sides, ranging ahead, and reported that they had come on no sign of water in any direction. So there was nothing for it but to accept the discomfort of a dry camp. They had water enough in their canteens for themselves and their cookery, but there was nothing for the horses, and the poor creatures, bone-dry from their labors of the afternoon, soon lost interest in the few blades of grass that they could find among the rocks. They stood around with their heads down and their eyes dull.

What talk there was that night around the campfire consisted of monosyllables and grunts. Every man was so thoroughly disgusted with himself that he wanted to take out his grievance on his neighbors. Themis was momently in fear that a fight would be started. But a natural reserve, and the fact that every man present was known to be an expert with a gun, deterred them.

So, finally, that wretched evening was closed by sleep. Only Si Bartlett was left awake to stand guard over them and prevent a visitation such as that which they had received the preceding night. He was to keep the watch until midnight, and then Red Norton would relieve him.

Silence dropped over the camp; even the dogs did not so much as whimper, so great was their weariness. But it was not an unbroken night of sleep. A wild shout wakened them, and then there was a rush of hoofs, snorting, and shrill neighing.

The campers jumped to their feet in time to see their entire herd of horses, with one exception, disappearing around the shoulder of a hill, and behind them was a wild figure of a man with long hair blown out behind his head and riding a beautiful stallion. Before a single shot could be fired, he had disappeared in the moonshine behind the hills, and the roar of hoofs tore away into distance, striking up loud echoes that slowly died away.

No man stirred to follow. To pursue such a flight on foot would be like attempting to climb a rainbow to the heart of heaven or putting a saddle on a snowslide. The horses were gone with the single exception of Mary Anne, and even she was working to follow as fast as her hobble would permit her.

Gloria caught her and brought the good mare back. On her return, she found that the rest of the men were gathered around Red Norton. He had been found thrown behind a rock, tied hand and foot with his own lariat so that he could not stir a muscle, and so thoroughly gagged that he had almost choked before he was delivered. He was still gasping and choking and clearing his throat. When he stood up, his face was purple with rage, his voice husky, and his wild eyes roved around in search of a victim.

But not a word of explanation would he offer. Only when Hank Jeffries rashly asked him if he had fallen asleep, a torrent of abuse broke forth.

"You hound!" thundered Red Norton. "D'you think I'm a fool? Fall asleep? I was as wide awake as I am now, wider awake than you could ever get. But when he. . . . I'll trail him if it takes me the rest of my life. But I'll trail him alone. I don't want no square-heads and half-wits along with me. I work better alone!"

It was too much for Hank Jeffries. His answer was like a flash of fire. But Themis stepped between them and struck down Norton's drawn gun. He stepped between them at a vital risk of his own life. It was something Gloria would never forget, that picture of her father, perfectly calm, his voice low and controlled.

"There's no use quarreling because we're beaten," he said. "There's no point in you being ashamed for what's happened, Norton. Any man in the world may be surprised by a fellow who seems to be able to turn himself into a shadow. If any one has cause to regret this night, I am he, I think. I'm going to pay every one of you his own price for the horse he has lost. You understand? And I'll do it without regret. I'm not dissatisfied with the men who have made this trip with me. The trouble has been that we've tried to follow a most extraordinary man as though he were a common mountaineer, whereas he's a genius in his own way. The next time we take the trail, we'll start out with just the same company. I wouldn't replace a single man who has made the trip. And I intend to start again, I assure you. If we are beaten a second time, I'll start a third. My patience is endless. I'm going to see this mysterious fellow face to face . . . unless the rest of you want to give up?"

The answer was a veritable roar of dissent. They would

stay with him. They would stay with such a generous and open-minded employer to the end of time. And they would sooner keep on the trail at their own expense than give it up, for their honor was pledged to find the Indian and hang him to a tree in proof that they had found him.

So much for the enthusiasm of the moment. But as the day began, the rising of the sun showed them the full extent of the catastrophe. Scores of weary miles lay between them and the village of Turnbull. They certainly could not carry with them a tithe of the equipment. It was agreed that Mary Anne, since Gloria resolutely refused to ride while the rest of the party walked, should be packed with enough provisions to last them for a quick, two-day march. Then the party should strike off, leaving one man behind to guard the saddles, the ammunition, and all the rest of the stores. But first he must be moved to water. They spent the day, until noon, sweating under heavy loads and carting their equipment five miles away to a small spring. There they left Dick Walker, who volunteered for the duty, and then started back for Turnbull village.

But there was one face in the party from which the eyes of Gloria never turned so long as she could watch him covertly, and that was big Red Norton. All the left side of his face was purple and swollen. Had he been struck with a club, or had that blow been delivered with the fist by a man of incredible strength? Surely strength so great could scarcely be coupled with. . . . She tried to combine the picture that was raised in her mind with the picture of the flowers that had been scattered around her two nights before. But here her imagination failed Gloria for the first time in her life.

Chapter Twenty-Four

"HERE LIES—"

Bad news has wings. But never did bad news travel more swiftly than on this occasion. Halfway to Turnbull, Themis and his following were met by a mounted party of a score of eager horsemen headed by the sheriff. From them, they learned that the entire herd of their horses had been found, in the evening of the day before, driven from the hills into the cañon near Hank Jeffries's house. At once there had sprung into the minds of the good men of Turnbull a picture of the entire Themis party murdered by the Indian, and they had struck swiftly into the mountains to bring vengeance, or to rescue if there were any survivors.

On the way back to Turnbull they heard the strange story of the pursuit of the man of mystery, and its conclusion. But should Dick Walker be permitted to stay alone in the hills, guarding what supplies remained, in the face of so terrible an enemy? The sheriff was assured that Dick Walker had made only one request—that he be permitted to stay where he was, alone. All that he wanted was an opportunity to meet the Indian face to face.

So they went on. If it had been another party, there would have been gibes in plenty and choruses of laughter at the expense of Themis and his men. But the stern faces of the five silenced all mirth.

Into Turnbull they descended, and there scattered, for they dreaded worse than death encountering the children of the village. What men dared not put a tongue to, children can turn into fluid laughter.

In fact, what they dared not say in the presence of the Themis party was freely talked of by the entire valley the next day. Six famous men had started out mounted on fine horses and equipped to the teeth to catch a single man, and that single man had sent them back on foot. It was a story with a Homeric ring. The Turnbull valley sent up a thunderous peal of laughter.

There was only one calm man in the valley, perhaps, and that man was John Hampton Themis. He could have pointed into his past to describe two months that had been entirely devoted to the trail of a man-killing lion in South Africa. He finally got that lion, and he would finally get the Indian. Of that he was quietly certain. In the meantime, he could do with less talk and more action.

First of all, he took Si Bartlett and Red Norton with saddle horses and several pack mules. They headed through the mountains to locate Dick Walker and their cache of equipment and provisions that must be brought back to Turnbull. Heading in a straight line, with no trail problems to untangle, they made the journey in less than two days, and by the bank of the runlet they found Dick Walker lying on his back with his arms thrown out crosswise, smiling up to the heavens with placid, open eyes, and with a purple hole in the center of his forehead. A revolver lay where it had fallen as he had released it, only a few inches from his fingers tips.

But the pile of equipment was intact, and beyond it they found the tracks of the Indian's bear—the unmistakable, huge tracks that not another creature in the mountains could have made. With the most casual scouting, they saw where the trail of Peter, the stallion, and Jerry, the bear, had approached the camp, apparently heading straight up to it, without an effort to conceal their coming. But perhaps they had come by night. Perhaps the fight had been by night. Perhaps it was the light of his own campfire that exposed poor Dick Walker to the fatal bullet.

They dug his grave deep and buried him with his eyes still open. Over the grave they rolled big boulders to make sure that the body could not be dug by wild beasts. Themis had a hammer and chisel. He carved into the face of the largest of the stones: **Here lies Richard Walker, murdered on this spot by treachery.**

When he had reached that point in his inscription, he turned to Si Bartlett and Red Norton. "Boys," he said, "I think I ought to find some kind thing to say about Dick and put it on this stone. Something that's true about him and fine about him."

The two were silent.

"Something like generosity," he said. "Was Dick generous? He gave the appearance of a liberal, free-swinging youngster."

Si Bartlett smiled. "Speaking of generosity," he said, "Dick was wasted up here in the mountains. He ought to have been down in some city. If one of the boys got broke, Dick would lend 'em money and charge half what he loaned as interest at the end of a month. He always had coin, but that was the way he handed it around. No, I wouldn't say that Dick was generous."

"He was faithful to his friends, though?" queried Themis.

"Ha! Suffolk," said Red Norton, "got interested in Dick when Dick was being tried for killing old Petersby. Hal sent out and brought in a fine lawyer and somehow got Dick loose from hanging . . . nobody ever knew just how. Then him and Dick went out on a prospecting trip. They got into some sort of an argument, and Dick shot him dead."

Themis rubbed his forehead thoughtfully. "Miserly, ungrateful, vicious," he said. "It seems there isn't very much that's good that we can say about him. But was he brave?"

"Brave? He didn't know what fear was," said Norton.

So it came about that the last of the inscription that Themis chiseled into the stone read: **He never turned his back on his enemy and died as he lived, facing danger.**

So they left Dick Walker, packed the mules with the goods, and started back toward the town of Turnbull. One thing remained self-evident. The Indian must die. His daring thefts, his cunning depredations, might be forgiven in a court of law because he had always attempted to make restitution of property, as in the case of the horses of the Themis party, or else he more than paid with furs for the articles he took. But how could he pay the price of a human life?

But they reached Turnbull, to find that the news they brought of the killing of Dick Walker was quite eclipsed by a recent happening in that village. Into the town, swarming as it was with armed men all keen to apprehend him, the Indian had come the night before, entered the house of Themis, found the room of the girl, and left upon her bed two priceless treasures—two perfect pelts of black foxes! An old trapper in a lifetime of work, if he is lucky, catches one such fox. But here were two beautiful skins whose value was simply what the fancy of a rich man chose to pay for them. They could not be represented by a market price. Furthermore, there was no doubt that the Indian had brought them. The prints of his moccasins were trailed back to a place in the hills where he had left Peter and the grizzly to come to the town. Then a serious effort had been made to trail him again on the return journey out of the town and into the hills. But here they had no luck. With consummate skill the wild man had made his return trail vanish into thin air, it seemed. They could not find a trace of him leaving the town.

Turnbull boiled with rage and excitement. There was not a youth old enough to bear arms who did not feel that his honor had been outraged because this daring fellow had ventured into the town to pay court to beautiful Gloria Themis. Again posses were organized, but this time there was no sudden pursuit and scouring through the hills, for they had learned the lesson, and they knew that a haphazard rush through the hills brought no result. The expedition of Themis might have failed, but, at least, all men admitted that his method of patience had been the only possible one.

Not a man would ride out to find the trail until the next day, and, in the meantime, to prevent a second visit of the Indian, a cordon was thrown around Turnbull. Literally scores of men and armed youths encircled the town. There was a perfect circle of campfires, so that the light of one stretched across and mingled with the light of another. The men sat in watches, relieving one another during the night and straining their eyes into the darkness. There was to be no hesitation, since the murder of Dick Walker was known. The instant they laid eyes upon a long-haired man, they were to challenge him, and, if he did not stop, they were to pour in their fire.

All of Turnbull remained wakeful. But, to show the gambling spirit of the townsmen and their faith in the power of the Indian to make himself invisible, odds were freely offered and found many takers at one to three that the wild man would walk through the line of fires safely and reach the home of his ladylove before the morning.

In fact, there was an inner cordon, as it might be called, stretched around the house of Themis itself. The place that he had rented to serve as headquarters was guarded by a dozen trusted men organized by Dude Wesson and Si Bartlett themselves.

In the house, like a small kernel inside so much guarding shell, sat Gloria, striving to read, but feeling a mist of excitement rising before her eyes again and again. In her lap lay one of those precious fox skins. It was like a mass of silk. It was dark as night. She could not help thinking of her face and white throat framed in the fur. But as she stroked it, she said to her father, who sat in the room with her for the sake of giving her more assurance: "Of course, if he's taken alive, I'll sell the skins for the best price I can get. In fact, I'll buy them myself at double the market value, and with that money he can retain the best lawyer in the country."

"*Hmm,*" said her father. "I never before knew that you had such uneasy nerves, Glory. You've not turned a page for half an hour."

"Oh, Dad," murmured Gloria, throwing the book aside, "I can't help pitying him. I can't help remembering the flowers he put around me. Wasn't that a beautiful thing to do?"

"*Hmm,*" grunted Themis again, "there is a poetic strain in many savages. They sacrifice to the Almighty one moment and eat the burnt flesh of the sacrifice the next. Don't think that this wild Indian is particularly remarkable in that respect. He shows his best talents on a trail."

"Dad," she cried with a show of anger, "when you've committed yourself to a theory, you're blind to everything else!"

"I simply keep my mind open to the facts," he said coldly, yet eying his daughter with a sharp anxiety. "This fellow doubtless has a fat squaw in the mountains. . . ."

"*Brr!*" shivered Gloria.

"Gloria," said her father, "tomorrow you start for New York, and from there you go on to Paris. The Swains are there now. They'll take care of you."

"I don't give a rap about Paris," said Gloria.

"Gloria!" he exclaimed.

"I don't care if I never see it," she insisted. "I'm going to stay here until I've seen the . . . Indian . . . face to face."

Themis bit his lip. "I'm going out to talk to Bartlett about something that's just occurred to me," he said. "I'll be back in a moment or two and look in to see if you're quieter. I really am afraid that you're growing hysterical, my dear. Good bye for a moment. And, of course, remember that there's no danger. No matter what these credulous townsmen may think, it's impossible for a man to transform himself into thin air and blow across the line of fires they've built."

He went out, and she heard his footsteps go down the hall. Then Gloria picked up the book again, settled herself firmly beside a light, and made her eyes follow the print. In a moment she was thoroughly into the story, and, when the door clicked behind her, she said quietly: "Is everything all right, Dad?" Then she jerked up her head and stared at the window, not daring to look behind her, for whoever had entered the room had come with a footfall as silent as the passage of the wind. There had been merely the stirring of a draft through her hair and the light click of the turning lock. Someone had entered and locked the door behind him. She was alone with the man.

Chapter Twenty-Five

AS FROM ANOTHER WORLD

In that moment of horror, she looked to the revolver that lay beside her on the table. No, if she reached for that, the Indian— if it were indeed he—would bound upon her from behind. But it could not be he. It must be John Themis who had returned so quickly. She forced herself to speak: "Dad!"

But the voice was a harsh, low whisper. Suddenly hysteria poured through her and supplied the place of strength. She leaped to her feet, scooped the gun from the table, whirled, and presented it at a tall man who stood just inside the door, a huge man, with sun-faded, brown hair that swept in a mass down to the nape of his neck, where it had been sawed off carelessly with a knife, a man whose skin was brown as an Indian's, indeed, but whose eyes were a bright and unmistakable Anglo-Saxon blue. He was dressed in a loose, buckskin shirt; rather, it was a buckskin sack with a hole through which his head had passed, and other holes where the sun-blackened, sinewy arms went through and were exposed to the shoulder. His trousers were of the same homemade pattern. They fitted closely about the ankles. On the man's feet were soft moccasins.

That was what she saw in the first wild glance. Then weakness swept through all her body. She slumped back into the chair. The gun slipped from her hand to the floor unheeded. It was a man of her own blood, a white man! No Indian that ever lived had looked out upon the world through such clear, blue eyes. But, as one terror left her, another took its place. Why had he come, and what would he do?

She scanned his face with a feverish interest, as one sweeps through the denouement of a strange story. She saw nobly molded features, a great, spacious forehead, an aquiline nose, a square, broad chin. Between his eyes there was incised a single deep wrinkle that seemed to say that this man had known pain and sorrow. As for his age, she guessed him at first to be thirty. But at a second glance something told her he was younger, much younger. Yet how could he be, if for six years he had defied all the manhunters of the Turnbull valley?

He had not stirred, meanwhile. He had not spoken. But he stood there with fire in his eyes, staring into her face. Then his glance lowered. He blushed through all the deep coats of tan, and raised his hand.

She saw for the first time that it was filled with moss, and on top of the moss was a cluster of pale blue flowers such as she had never seen before.

"I knew that there were no flowers in this place," he said, "so I brought these, but it was a long way, and they died. Perhaps they need the snow."

Fear had been like a cold mantle on Gloria, but, when she heard his voice, when she saw the flowers in those strong hands, the chill left her. Instead, she was poured full of excitement like a brimmed cup.

He crossed the room. Even in that moment she noted that his step made no sound on the floor, no creaking of the boards. He dropped to a knee before her as she shrank away, and offered the withering blossoms.

"You are afraid," he said sadly. "But I tell you truly that they can do you no harm. I found them by a stream of snow water. There was a thick cluster of them. They were like water themselves reflecting the sky. You see what a pale blue?"

"I am not afraid . . . of them," murmured Gloria. "May I take them?"

"Yes, yes," he said eagerly. "And if you close your eyes and look into the darkness hard, you will see the mountain where they grew. It is just below timberline. The snow is still beneath the trees. The air is sweet with the pines. And the head of the mountain goes up above into the sky. At night, it touches the stars."

She took the moss into her lap. The flowers were faded, indeed, but all that she could see of them was a mist of blue, a pale blue like when the sun is in the middle of heaven.

He knelt still with his hand outstretched. His glance went up from the blossoms to her eyes. The shock of those meeting glances sent a tingle through her.

"Who are you? What are you?" said Gloria.

"I am Tom Parks," he answered.

It was like giving the free wind a name. She could not hold back a faint, excited smile.

"I have heard them speak your name near the campfire," he said. "You are Gloria."

She nodded.

"It is a good name to say over and over," he said gravely. "I have said it in the middle of the night, aloud. It brings up your face."

A tide of deep crimson swept over the face of Gloria. She set her teeth, but still her heart fluttered.

"Has that angered you?" he asked, and all the time his glance was prying anxiously at her face.

She shook her head, for at that moment she could not have spoken.

"You see," he went on in that same musical, deep voice, "I

cannot tell what words will do. For ten years I have not spoken to a man or a woman or even a child, so I cannot tell what words will do. I cannot tell what words should be used to make people happy. But if I knew . . . ah, if I knew, Gloria . . . I should take a thousand and a thousand words. I should make them into songs. I should sing them for you until you smiled and smiled and smiled!"

He had thrown back his head, and the great, strong throat trembled with his emotion. Gloria looked on him with a sort of frightened wonder and scared delight. Outside the houses were the voices of men who were hunting him. They would snuff out his life like a candle. Yet here he was making love to her a dozen feet from them, and speaking as she had never before heard men speak. At eighteen Gloria had seen wise men grow silly. A pretty face performs strange feats of alchemy.

"But, since I cannot talk," said the wild man, "I have brought something you may understand better than my words. It has made me happy. Perhaps it will make you happy, too."

Then he took from a leather pouch at his side a little, long-tailed, tree squirrel. The instant it was liberated, the tiny creature ran from his hand up his arms, climbed the ends of his hair, and sat on his head, looking at her out of twinkling eyes. Gloria caught her breath.

"He has a small head, but he is very wise," said Tom Parks. "He brings me a present everyday out of the trees. He is never quiet. He is always doing something. But, when you whistle like this, he will always stop and come to you."

He whistled softly, a low, faint note, and the squirrel whirled, climbed to his shoulder, darted down onto his hand, and stood up, looking into his face. Gloria clasped her hands with delight. Girls at eighteen may be very wise, but, after all, they are only girls of eighteen.

"Call him," said Tom, entranced with happiness as he saw her pleasure.

She tried the whistle, and she learned the note almost at once. The tree squirrel twisted about, eyed her with an anxious interest, and then ran down the leg of Tom Parks and climbed up her dress to her lap. There he sat up and regarded her with deep interest. Tom Parks gave her a pine nut. She offered it to the little fellow between the tips of her dainty fingers, and he took it in his paws like a child and sat up peeling the brittle shell away and then nibbling the kernel. The tip of his tail was curled up over his head.

"When winter comes," said Tom Parks, "and you are alone in the evenings, when the wind is shouting through the mountains and the cave is cold in spite of the fire, you will be glad to have him. He will make you smile."

"But how can I take him?" said Gloria. "You will be lonely and unhappy without him."

"No, no," he protested. "You must see that, if I know he is with you, I shall be ten times happier, for, when you see him, you will think of me. Is that true?"

"I could not help it," said Gloria.

He laughed silently in his happiness. "I knew that! I knew that!" he exclaimed.

A door closed in the distance. Instantly he was on his feet, and his bigness, his alertness, alarmed her.

"I must go now," he said. "Your father will be coming back. No, that is not he."

He had listened intently, while he spoke, and, although she heard nothing at first, she presently made out a footfall going through the house. Gloria slipped between Tom and the door.

"You must not go!" she exclaimed. "Don't you see that

the house is surrounded by men? Beyond them, there is another circle around the town? How you came through them tonight, I can't imagine!"

"I didn't come into town tonight," he replied quietly. "I have been in this house since yesterday."

Gloria gasped.

"In this house?"

"I was afraid to wait and see you yesterday," said Tom Parks, "so I've been lying in a room upstairs where no one comes. There were no trails in the dust on the floor when I went in. I guessed that no one would come while I was there. And I have laid there trying to make myself brave to come and see you."

"You were afraid . . . of me?" said Gloria.

"I should have known," he said humbly, "that because you are so beautiful, you are kind, also. But I have seen men do strange things. How could I be sure that a woman is different? You will not believe what I have seen men do!"

"Tell me," said Gloria.

With all her heart she wanted to bid him to be gone, or else find some way of sheltering him there and warning him of his danger. But to part with him was like parting with a rare treasure that may be held for a moment but not kept. The time of their meeting was like bubbles of foam, melting away every instant, never to be repeated.

"I cannot tell you everything," he said, "but once I saw a man tie a horse to a tree because the horse was tired and could not pull the wagon up the hill. He beat that horse with a whip. He beat that horse until the blood came . . . and the horse was helpless!"

"Oh," cried Gloria, "how terrible! And what did you do?"

He stiffened and knotted his hands, and in that gesture there was a connotation of Herculean power.

"I climbed into the tree," he said. "Then I dropped out of the branches. I tied him, and I beat him with his own whip!"

She had heard that story with many strange embroiderings.

"Once," he went on, "I saw a hunter come to a mountain sheep that had broken its leg in a fall. He stabbed it in the throat and watched it bleed to death, slowly, slowly."

"Ah," murmured Gloria in horror, "what did you do then?"

"I turned and ran away," he said, his face dark with rage and disgust. "I did not dare to stay near, because I wanted to take him in my hands and kill him. I wanted to kill him little by little, as he was killing the sheep. But there are other things I have seen men do. I have a horse that comes to me when I speak to him. He follows me when I walk. He is sad when I leave him, and, when I come again, he sees me at a great distance and comes to me with much neighing and calling. He dances around me. And then he hunts in my pouch for something I have brought. He will run with me until his heart breaks and still keep his ears pricking to show that his love for me is greater than his weariness!" He paused. Tears were in his eyes. "But that horse," he said savagely, "a man had tied to a post and was about to shoot. That very horse . . . Peter! Can you believe that?"

She could not answer. His wild anger, his profound pity, and his overwhelming love, were like unknown countries to her. She was amazed.

"When I had seen men do such things," he said, "how could I tell what even you would do . . . Gloria?"

He made a little pause before her name and after it, and he spoke the name itself with an intonation that made it music. She was looking into a mirror and seeing herself transformed, glorified.

"I lay by the fire," he said, "and listened to your voice. It was to me . . . to me . . . like the falling of fragrant flowers. And again, it was like a look up, through the trees, into the sky, into the stars. And still I was afraid that, when I met you, I would find you like other men. But the moment I came inside this room and into your presence I knew the truth. I knew that you were as good as you are beautiful."

"Hush!" said Gloria, and raised her hand.

She saw him wince. Then he stood statue-still.

"I knew it," he murmured at last. "Words cannot say what I wish them to say. They are made out of breath. I speak and speak and speak, but I take nothing from what is within me. There is still more than ever within me . . . like all that lies between two great mountains and all that lies beyond them."

"I cannot listen to you," Gloria said faintly.

"I have made you unhappy?"

"Not . . . not unhappy, but too happy, too sadly happy. Do you see?"

"I shall not try to understand," he said humbly.

She passed a hand across her forehead to wipe the spell away, but, when she looked at him again, it was unchanged. He still seemed like a young god out of another world, a world lost to all except himself, into which she could not follow him.

"I have found the thing at last," she said suddenly. "I shall keep you here in this room . . . yes, in this very room . . . until morning. Then, when they have left the fires, you will have a better chance to get away."

He looked at her in amazement. "You don't know them, then," he said. "You don't know these men. They hate me. But how have I harmed them? Still, they hate me. If they knew you helped me, they would kill you, Gloria, even you!"

"They would never touch a woman, not the worst of them," said Gloria.

But he shook his head. "I have seen them torture dumb animals," he said, "and a woman can speak. Men who kill sheep would kill women. I know! And so I leave you, Gloria, before they come. But I shall come again."

"You must not. They watch me in order to catch you. Since Dick Walker was killed . . . oh, I know that you killed him because he deserved death, but the others cannot understand."

"I did not kill that man," he said calmly.

She stared at him. But could any man lie with such a steady face?

"They found him dead," she said slowly. "And they found the trail of a horse and a bear near him."

"I came to that place and saw him on his back with a hole in his forehead," said Tom with a shudder. "I went away quickly. It is a terrible thing to see a dead man. I have seen two."

"Ah," murmured Gloria, "it is true, then? He was killed by some other man?"

"Yes."

"Then," she cried in excitement, "don't you see what you must do? You must go back to that place. You must find the murderer. You must bring him to Turnbull. That is the only serious crime they can charge against you. Money can settle all the rest, and I have money."

He was bewildered, fumbling for her meaning. "Do you mean," he said at last, "that, if I find him and bring him here, they will no longer hunt me?"

"I mean that," said Gloria. "And if. . . ."

She stopped for a familiar step came hastily down the hall, stopped at her door. The knob was turned under his hand.

"What the deuce, Gloria?" cried the father. "Have you locked yourself in?"

Chapter Twenty-Six

THE BATTLE OF THE NIGHT

Gloria was rooted to the floor with horror. She should not have allowed him to stay until the trap had closed. Before she could rally her wits, Tom Parks turned to her with a smile and a gesture which, if it meant anything, declared that there was no serious danger immediately ahead. She saw him turn the key in the lock. The door opened. Then, suddenly, fear for her father leaped into her brain. There was a shrill, involuntary cry of warning, but what happened came before Themis could understand and defend himself.

As he stepped into the room, he was seized from the side, pitched headlong to the floor on his face with as much ease as though he had been a child, and Tom Parks, leaping into the hall, paused to turn the lock from the outside. She heard it click. Then John Hampton Themis sprang to his feet with his revolver in his hand, bewildered and furious. He cast at his daughter one baffled glance. Then he leaped for the door. When he found it locked, his shout of warning rang through the house. Next, a bullet from his revolver shattered the lock, and he burst into the hall.

As for Tom Parks he had not fled headlong down the hall. He turned into the door of the room next to that of Gloria. He found a window open and stood beside it, waiting. Beyond the window he could see armed men standing, regarding the house with a sober interest, for they had half heard the cry of

Gloria. But when the revolver shot of Themis was heard, then the crash of the door as it was flung open, and last his shout of rage and alarm in the hall, they waited no longer outside the house but rushed pell-mell around the corner to enter it and get at the root of the trouble.

That was the movement for which Tom had waited. Instantly he was out the window and had dropped with the lightness of a cat to the ground. There, in the deep shadow of the house, he waited an instant. He was unarmed, and his hands ached for a gun. But when he came near the haunts of men, the great enemy, he purposely left weapons behind him, because he never knew when the temptation would become stronger than his ability to resist.

That second of thoughtfulness gave him a course, however. In another moment the lines of watchers around the town would know that he was inside its limits, and, by simply turning around and facing the village instead of the outer night from which they had expected him to come, they would have him sealed in a trap.

He raced to the rear of the next house on the street. In the corral beside the barn there were horses, but none for his purpose. He could tell that even by their outlines in the darkness. He went on like a flash to the next corral and scanned a huddle of horses standing in a corner. He looked for a head, not for a body, and finally he saw what he wanted—a small, compact, bony head, with short, sharp ears. That was his horse.

He sprang to the barn, wrenched the door open, and, on a row of pegs inside, he found bridles, saddles, and blankets. But he only took a bridle. Even for that there was barely time. Voices were beginning to shout here and there in the outer night. Perhaps the whole circle of the campfires had been alarmed by this time.

He came out again. The horses in the corner of the corral split apart and scattered, snorting.

"Halloo!" shouted the voice of a man from the house in front of the barn. "Hello, out there! What's up?"

Tom made no answer. He had just succeeded in cornering the horse with the finely made head. It was a disappointingly small animal—not comparable with Peter, of course. But he stayed with his choice.

"Look here!" roared the man of the house, now excited. "What's up out there? Bill, come along and let's take a look."

Tom heard the voice of Bill answer. But now he was working at the head of the horse. The stubborn little brute kept his jaws locked and refused to admit the bit. He put two fingers into the side of the beast's mouth and dug them down into the gums. That forced the mouth open, and instantly the bridle was on and slipped over the ears of the mustang.

After that, he did not wait to secure the throatlatch. He sprang to the back of his horse—and instantly found that his hands were filled with an argument of another nature, for the bronco tipped into the air and came down crooked. For thirty seconds it bucked with a wild enthusiasm and a cunning intelligence that proved it to be an old hand. But there was no unseating Tom Parks. He had learned to ride Peter in the mountains without a saddle. He had a grip with his knees almost sufficient to break the ribs of his mount, so he clung on his back.

"By heaven!" roared one of the men who was running toward the corral. "It's somebody on Sideways!"

Sideways was demonstrating the aptness of that name by a series of bucks from side to side delivered with the violence of a snapping whip and the speed of striking fists.

"Shoot for him. Try for his head!" cried one of the men.

Tom gritted his teeth. It is impossible to sit a bucking

horse without carrying one's head high. He could not duck and flatten himself along the back of the mustang. A gun clanged, and a bullet sang wickedly close to his ear.

"Look out for Sideways, though," cautioned the other. "I'll watch the gate. We'll get him."

Suddenly Sideways came out of the bucking humor and decided to try running, as horses will do, apparently thinking that they can run out from under the burden on their backs. So Sideways bolted and made, naturally enough, straight for the corral gate. A frightened yell went up from the man who had posted himself there. Two guns banged in close succession, but the shots flew idly overhead, for the instant the mustang stopped bucking and began to run, Tom had flattened himself along its neck.

They reached the gate. He twitched Sideways to one side and aimed him at the fence. Did the little brute know how to jump, and could he manage it with such a weight on his back? The question was quickly answered. Sideways went for the fence with a grunt of anger, reared, and skimmed it like a bird. Yells of amazement greeted the feat.

He landed in his stride and was off racing. Tom let him get past two barns. Then he twitched him to the side and hurried him across the village, leaving behind him the line of campfires with the excited men milling around them, black, misshapen silhouettes.

The village of Turnbull was long and narrow, like most Western towns. In an instant he was across the main street, had plunged Sideways down an alley, and came in view of the opposite campfires. Everywhere was shouting and confusion and the gleam of the fires upon guns.

Coming out of the black night, he was dazzled by that glare of many lights. He could not choose or pick. He simply made for the first gap between the fires while a wild yell of excitement and fear went tingling up to greet him. Then the air was filled with the din of guns.

"We were onto fifty yards away," goes the old hunting story. "Every one of us was a good shot. At that range who could miss? We put forty bullets into that grizzly before he hit the brush, and we lost him. Yes, sir, he was a walking lead mine before he disappeared." Yet, when the bear was found dead the next day, there was a solitary slug in him, and he had died from the effects of that one. What had made fifty bullets or more fly astray? Simply that fever of nervousness that makes the hand, so steady in firing at a target, quiver just a little in firing at a living thing. And hands that shook when they fired at a bear would certainly be tremulous when they attempted to kill this terrible wild man who came upon them by surprise from an unexpected direction. Just an instant, and the flying horse had carried him—long, bare arms and long, flying hair and all—out of the darkness of the houses and into the midst of the guards.

Of a hundred shots, not one struck home or even grazed the target. There was one flurry of wild shooting, and then Sideways, running with wild speed in his terror, dipped into a swale in a hollow and was lost to view. The others rushed to the edge of the swale to get in another volley, but by that time Sideways had put a precious 100 yards between him and the foremost of the sentinels.

The last volley flew wildly astray, and then the blanketing night closed on them, and Tom headed for the hills.

What a blessing it was that the noise fell away behind him, every stride of the good little horse making it dimmer. He had no occasion to regret the selection of Sideways, bucking and all, for every inch of his scant fifteen hands was all horse. He was a bundle of strength and nervous energy, and it was all loosed in that wild horse to get away from the town.

But now Tom Parks drew the mustang back to a more moderate gait. A furlong of sprinting exhausts a man as much as a mile of running. Sideways had been taxed by fear and anger and a racing gait all at once. It was no wonder that his sides were heaving as Tom brought him down to a canter. He began to talk as he alone knew how to talk to a dumb beast. What wonder that he could, when only dumb beasts had been near to listen for years? In a moment the tremor had left the body of Sideways, and under the persuasion of that gentle voice and the hand that stroked his sleek, strong neck, he began to raise his head, and one ear pricked forward. It warmed the heart of Tom to see.

In the meantime, all was not well. There had been a pale semicircle of light over the eastern hills. Now from that glow was born a great, full moon that filled the valley with swarthy shadows. It was not so bad as the all-revealing sun, but it was bad enough. For one thing, he had come out from Turnbull on the side farthest from the direction that led toward Peter and safety. For another thing, there was a dull and increasing roar of hoofs in his rear. Tom knew that the battle of the night was by no means ended.

Chapter Twenty-Seven

TOM MAKES A PROMISE

They were coming fast and hard on his heels. Every man in the village who had a horse had flung himself into the saddle. But most had fallen to the rear. There remained a round dozen of well-mounted men who had pushed on. To be sure, their horses had the burden of saddles to carry, a thing from which Sideways was freed, but the little mustang had in Tom a greater weight than an average rider and saddle combined. Moreover, he had used up the blossom of his strength in that first wild burst of running and bucking. Tom shrewdly suspected that Sideways, with his short legs and his sturdy frame, would be better fitted for a long and steady run than for the arduous labors of a swift chase.

The thing to do was to get to Peter. Five minutes of that matchless speed would leave the posse staggering and floundering behind him in the night. But how to reach Peter was the problem.

He decided, first of all, to keep straight on until the hills were a screen behind him. Then he would angle to the right and speed around until he could break across toward the opposite side of the valley where Peter had been left. What he needed now was a burst of speed to carry him into those hills as soon as possible.

Tom called to Sideways, and the good little horse lowered his nose, stretched out his neck, and raced like a champion

175

until the steep hill shadows pushed past him and he was shut from the view of the pursuers.

Chance came to the help of Tom then. He saw before him half a dozen little ravines opening like so many funnels into the heart of the hills. How could the pursuers pick the right avenue for following him? He took the one that led most directly to the right, and, still keeping Sideways at top speed, he tore down it. Behind him, as the mustang raced, he heard the roar of hoofs and the shouting of men as they drove past the entrance to the cañon. But Tom did not slacken the pace even after this assurance that the posse had gone wrong. What he vitally needed was a sufficiently big gap between him and the others so that, when he chose, he could angle back across the Turnbull valley.

But he rode fast simply to make surety doubly sure, as men will do sometimes. It was twenty minutes before he decided that he could safely cut back. Then he let Sideways, now badly blown by all this sprinting, fall to a swaying canter that, he knew, the little horse could maintain all day. So he drifted back through the hills and came out on the plain once more.

He scanned it eagerly right and left, but over the rolling ground, now white with moonshine, he saw no dark forms of hurrying horsemen. He let Sideways continue at the same pace. Then, from a slight elevation, he caught sight of the wide, bright body of the river flowing through the distance ahead of him. They could swim that to safety.

But, as he sent Sideways ahead at a slightly freshened pace, a change of the wind brought an ominous sound to his ear. He swung sharply about, and he saw, streaking across the crest of a low knoll, a compact body of half a dozen mounted men, aimed at him at full speed. For a moment he was stunned. Then he saw the only possible explanation. Those who led the party that first pursued him must have guessed that his retreat into the hills was only a feint, for he had always made his descents into Turnbull valley from the opposite side of the valley. So they had split their party into sections. One plunged after him into the hills, and he had heard them go by on a false scent. The other had roamed along the foothills to see if they could find him as he doubled back. That strategy had succeeded. There they were coming with their comparatively fresh horses that had been kept in hand all this time. And here was he with a weary mount!

But there was nothing for it save to make Sideways sprint again and head straight on for the river. That was what he did, working himself well forward toward the withers of the little horse so that his weight would be a lesser burden at great speed. Then, with hand and voice, he shot Sideways ahead.

The brave little horse answered with all the strength in his body and, what was more important, with all the power in his soul. He ran until his legs were numb and his lungs on fire, but still those swiftly shooting shadows behind him gained and gained. In vain Tom tried to angle up the river for a more favorable crossing place. The instant he started to travel at a slant, the pursuit gained with appalling speed. Still, when he straightened the little horse fully for the river, they gained again.

Even if he gained the water, they could reach the bank, and, sitting quietly in the middle, they could riddle him with bullets better aimed than the few that they now, from time to time, sent whizzing after him. But shooting from horseback is a fine art in itself. If he, Tom Parks, had a rifle with him, he would show them how it was done. If he had six shots, he would empty six saddles for them and hunt the rest of them back across the valley as fast as they had hunted him. But his hands were empty, and he could only groan, then throw all his anguish into the voice that called on Sideways for more speed.

Still somewhere in the valiant recesses of his heart, Sideways found mysterious stores of energy upon which he called. Still he answered that voice, until he was reeling in his stride. Yet the posse closed suddenly upon him. Now the water flashed just before them. Headlong he drove the mustang at it. A cloud of silver spray was dashed up by the hoofs of the horse. He lunged in, and the water closed over them.

That instant Tom thrust himself from the mustang and kicked off underwater, swimming below the surface and with all his might. He swam until his lungs threatened to burst. Then his hands touched bottom. He drew himself to the edge of the river. In a tangle of weeds he thrust his nose and eyes above the surface and saw the drama that followed.

The horsemen of the posse, as he had expected, had halted on the bank. Their rifle butts were pitched into the hollows of their shoulders. For an instant they scanned the silver surface of the Turnbull for sight of the man they wanted. But, imagining that the mustang in some way concealed the master, they poured a volley of lead at that gallant head where Sideways was struggling on across the current.

Tom, with an aching heart, saw poor Sideways sink beneath the surface. Then, to his soul of souls, he made a vow that for the sake of Sideways he would be kinder to all horses—to all dumb creatures—if his own life were spared from this crisis.

But there was now a shout of wonder from the posse as they saw the head of the horse go down while still no man appeared in the water.

"I guess I nailed him just as he hit the water," said one

voice. "Sure looked to me like I landed him. Look down the stream a ways, boys. Maybe you'll see him floating."

"If he went down, he won't be up for days," said another. "Why didn't you hold up and wait when you seen we had him, Bill?"

"A fox like that?" said Bill. "Any way of getting him was good enough for me. But I'd sure like to see his face. Hunt down the stream, boys. This current might wash him into the shallows."

They drifted down the stream a little, but Tom dared not move from his place. There he lay in the numbing water and heard them come back.

"The thing to do," said the quiet voice of John Hampton Themis, "is for you fellows to go back to the town and tell what has happened. Tell 'em that we've run the rat into the water. I'll stay out here and watch the place."

"D'you think that he's living and breathing down under the water, Mister Themis?" asked another with a chuckle.

"I don't know what to think," answered Themis. "I only know that it will be a strange thing if a man such as he seems to be has been disposed of as easily as this. We've only accounted for one of his lives tonight."

This brought another good-natured laugh. They were in high spirits. The heart of Tom raged in him as he listened to their laughter. Presently, however, they agreed with Themis. They bade him farewell and assured him that he would not have a lonely watch. Others would come out from the village in the night to see the place, and in the morning they would all come out and drag the river by sunlight.

"And watch yourself, Mister Themis," they said. "The rat might come out of the water and sink his teeth into you."

So, with more laughter, they rode on. The great silence of the night fell over the place. There was only the light whisper of the river against its banks.

"Strange . . . very strange," Tom heard Themis say, speaking just above him.

Then the noise of the horse of Themis retreated down the river a little and Tom dared to raise his head above the weeds. Down the bank he saw Themis disappear below a knoll. Quickly he worked himself out of the slime. On the grassy bank he rolled himself. He worked all his muscles convulsively two or three times to restore, in part, his deadened circulation and the vitality that the chill of the water had sapped. Then he rose to his knees.

Instantly he heard the sound of the hoofs of the horse as the solitary sentinel started to return. He must find shelter somewhere, and there was only one possibility. That was a growth of shrubs not more than a foot high, far too low and too thin to give him actually a shelter, but they must serve his purpose. He lay among them, face down, because there is nothing that, for some mysterious reason, so attracts the eye as the human face, even by night. He could only pray that his body might not be distinguishable among the shadows of the shrub. To reinforce his hope, he felt that the eye of the watcher would be chiefly employed on the bright surface of the river.

Back came the noise of hoofs. It was aimed directly at him. So straight came the noise of the approach that he turned his head toward it, and it was as he feared. Themis was letting the horse wander on straight toward the patch of shrubbery. Perhaps he would let the animal walk straight through it.

Tom gathered his legs a little under him. If it came to the worst, he must attack in the face of that gleaming rifle that was balanced across the pommel of Themis's saddle. He waited, his teeth set, his eyes gleaming, his toes digging in to gain a purchase in case that leap must be made.

Still the nodding head of the horse came on, while Themis sat the saddle looking toward the water. A yard away—suddenly the horse stopped, snorted, then bounded to the side while Themis, with an exclamation of surprise, lowered his rifle and drew heavily on the reins.

There was no escape now for Tom. The horse had seen him. The man would see him in another instant. He came out of the shrubs with a rush. He saw the rifle swung up. Then he leaped for the rider and, with upflung left hand, touched the muzzle of the gun of Themis. It discharged its contents just beside Tom's ear. Then, his lunge carrying him on and up, one hand fell on the shoulder of Themis, another circled his neck.

Themis was torn from the saddle and brought heavily to the earth. Half stunned by the fall, he allowed the rifle to be jerked from his nervous hands. He was forced upon his back. In a trice, hands and feet were tied. Then he was wrenched to a sitting posture and found himself confronting the muddy, dripping figure that stood there, rifle in hand.

"You are still alive," said a stern voice. "You are her father, and therefore you are still alive. But the others, when I find them, shall die. They murdered the poor horse while it swam in the water. How had that horse harmed them? They shall die as the horse died. Tell them that when they come. I have let them hunt me like a dog through the mountains. When they come again, tell them that I shall shoot, and I never miss."

He threw rifle and revolver far off into the river, while the frightened horse fled, neighing. Then he ran to the edge of the river and dived into it.

Themis, looking after him, saw the water close above him with hardly a ripple to break the surface. He came up far toward the center of the stream, swimming strongly, with his face buried. He reached the farther bank. He climbed the shore and stood a moment, a dripping, shining figure. Then he struck across country with a long, free stride and was lost in the moon haze.

Chapter Twenty-Eight

GLORIA IS UNYIELDING

"We start this afternoon," said John Hampton Themis with the cheery finality of one who expects opposition but pretends that he does not dream of it. "I have completed the arrangement, my dear. New York and then a boat for Paris."

But Gloria, for a moment, merely tapped her foot and watched him. She seemed to be more interested in him than in any effect this statement might have upon her.

"You'll have a beautiful time, Dad," she said. "I wish you joy."

"And you," said Themis, "will have your Paris . . . as much of it as you can stand."

"Paris?" she said in mock surprise. "Paris for me? No, no, Dad. I've finally become convinced that you are right. I'm too young to do justice to Paris, or for Paris to do justice to me. I'll wait. I don't care how many years it is . . . but I'll wait for another time."

Themis cleared his throat, began a sentence, and changed his mind. "Just what are your plans?" he asked.

"I haven't seen nearly enough of Turnbull valley," she said. She whistled softly. A tiny little form whisked across the room, ran up her skirt, and perched upon her knee. It was the tree squirrel. She began to pet it idly.

"So you stay here?" asked Themis, staring fixedly at the squirrel.

"Yes, thank you. I've barely become acclimated, you see. It would be a shame to leave now. And for my part, I don't see how you can leave, Dad."

"No?"

"Certainly not. Every man in the valley expects you to stay here until you've caught the wild man . . . the Indian, as you call him."

Themis flushed. "I freely admit," he said, "that I was in error. He's white. As for staying here to capture him, you've surely not forgotten what happened the other night?"

"In what way?"

"He had me helpless under his gun, and he let me live."

"People may say that you're afraid to face him again."

Once more Themis flushed. "I'll have to endure that," he said quietly. "My friends, I hope, will not believe it. As for the others . . . well, no matter what they think, I can't stay on the trail of a man who had me at his mercy, then let me go after I had hunted him for his life." He sighed, and his glance probed the distance with a singular regret. "How he did it," he said, "I still can't understand. I look back on it, and it still doesn't seem possible that any human being could have been capable of such activity. It was like the rush of a tiger . . . like the rush of a tiger, on my honor."

He rose and paced the room hurriedly. His voice was low, while speaking of that incredible thing. "He must have been flat on the ground when the horse shied, Glory. But he came off from it, with a bound as though he were made of rubber. And the second leap had him at me. I'll never forget that face. His teeth were glinting in the moonshine. His long hair was tangled with mud and dirt. He looked like a devil. All that happened before I could get in a shot." He shook his head. "When he caught my shoulders . . . gad, his fingers seemed iron! The flesh is still black and blue." He rubbed that shoulder meditatively.

"Frankly," he continued, "I'm afraid of him. I'd hate like the devil to have to trail him. But the worst of it is that, while I might go with a gun to shoot him, he'll not take his chances to shoot in turn, because I'm your father. And that, Glory, brings me to the crux of the matter."

She nodded quietly, but she drew the tree squirrel suddenly close to her.

"Glory," he said slowly, "you want to stay here because of that wild man. Tell me truly."

"That's the exact truth," said Gloria. "You've seen through me, Dad."

He shuddered. There was such pain in his face that she lowered her eyes, unable to watch him.

"Gloria," he said sadly, "it's my fault, I know. It's entirely my fault. I've let you grow up doing as you please. I've spoiled you terribly. Now you'll fight for your own way. It's impossible for you to give up anything you want."

She slipped out of the chair and went to him and took his hands.

The squirrel ran up the back of the chair and perched on the top of it, peering at her with its bright little eyes.

"Don't say that, Dad," she pleaded. "I know you've spoiled me, but there's hardly a thing in the world that I wouldn't do for you, if you seriously asked me."

"Except to leave Turnbull with me now?"

She bowed her head.

"Glory!" he cried in agony. "Do you mean it? Even if I beg you, as I do now, to come with me?"

"Oh, Dad," she answered, her eyes filling with tears, "if you only would ask proof of me in some other way. If I could only show you how dear you are to me, Dad, and what I would suffer for you. But this one thing. . . ."

He released her hands and stepped to the window, breathing deeply. Then he forced himself to face her again. It seemed to Gloria that he had aged by ten years in the past day.

"It means a tragedy if you stay here," he said. "My dear, we all feel that we know ourselves better than others can possibly know us. But don't you think we may sometimes be wrong? I think I understand you, Glory. And I tell you that if you see this wild man again while your brain is still in a riot from that first meeting, you'll lose control of yourself. Before you know it, you'll be married, and your life will be ruined."

She paused to show that she was taking all his words to heart. "Will you listen to my viewpoint?" she said at last.

"Of course," said Themis. "I want you to talk . . . talk about everything. Get it out of your heart and into words if you can."

"Suppose you look at it in this way, then. If I never see him again, if I never talk with him again, the thought of him will haunt me. Dad, this room is filled with him. He was here five minutes, but he has left something in every corner of the room. The sound of his voice has never run out of my ears. I keep seeing his face . . . sometimes I've turned around short in going down the hall because it seemed to me as if he were coming behind me with that silent step of his. Do you understand how I feel now?"

"Glory," he said, "let's take another angle. If you stay here, the man's devotion to you will bring him down to the town again. When he comes down, he'll be caught. He escaped once, you know by how small a margin. A second time he can't escape. And when he's caught, he'll be hanged for murder. Nothing can prevent that."

"It's not true!" cried Gloria. "He told me with his own voice that he did not kill Dick Walker."

"I believe him as thoroughly as you do," said Themis. "But that does not spoil the case against him. He had a motive for killing Walker. His trail was seen going there. What more could be needed? He'd be hanged, Gloria."

"An innocent man! Oh, Dad, it's too horrible! I'll find some means of preventing it."

"That's a blind hope. If you really are fond of the wild man . . . of Tom Parks, as you call him . . . the best thing is to leave Turnbull valley, because, so long as you stay here, you're the bait for a trap that may catch him."

"He has gone himself to find the murderer of Walker."

"But the trail has been wiped out by the rains before this. You mustn't console yourself with absolute impossibilities, my dear."

"Oh," she cried, bewildered, "there will be some way!"

Her father shrugged his shoulders. "Besides," he said, "even if he dodges the law for a time, he'll eventually be captured."

"They've failed for six years."

"What's six years to the law? It will wait a lifetime. Eventually it wins. It has forever. It uses a million hands. One man cannot stand against it, particularly since Parks has become notorious. Manhunters will come from all parts of the West. They'll run his trail through every month of the years. Finally he'll go down. Gloria, if you were to attach yourself to him, you'd attach yourself to a doomed cause."

He saw, by the way her head went back, that he had made a wrong step.

"Dad!" she exclaimed. "Do you want me to leave the ship because the rats have left it? Do you want me to be a coward?"

He gritted his teeth. "Think of your friends, Gloria."

"He's worth all of them."

"How could he meet them?"

187

"They would be honored by a syllable from him, or else they're not worthy to speak with him. But don't you see, Dad, I only want to meet him once more and make sure? Perhaps it will be different when I see him again. The glamour will be gone."

He shook his head sadly. "Not with you, Gloria. It needs more time than you'll have between meetings. No man has ever meant anything to you. And now you'll cling to this first enthusiasm. . . ." Suddenly he stopped talking. He went to her and took her in his arms. "My dear," he said, "if I were a religious man, I should pray God to help us both do right in this thing."

Chapter Twenty-Nine

TACTICS OF THE TRAIL

When Tom Parks, well before sunup, reached that cleft in the hills where he would find the stallion and big Jerry, he sent a long screaming whistle over the trees and listened until he heard faintly a whinny in the distance. After that, he did not wait for either the horse or the bear to come. They would find him and wait.

The good men of Turnbull were mustering and making ready for another hunt. But it would still be a short interval before sunup and their start, so Tom lay down in a corner behind a rock, where the wind could not get at him, and was instantly asleep.

For two hours he lay without stirring, and, when he wakened, the fresh light of dawn filled the sky. Beside him was Peter, cropping the grass. In the near distance was the bulk of Jerry, paying his attention to a colony of ants. He had already devoured the contents of half a dozen ant hills. Now he was demolishing a seventh nation, but, at the voice of Tom, he whirled and came with his thundering but swift stride across the clearing.

Peter began to sweep around the returned master in swift loops, flirting his heels into the air and shaking his head, bucking and gamboling more in air than on firm ground. As for Jerry, he stood upon his hind legs, viewed the master carefully, then went around him, sniffing the strange man scents that he found, and growling terribly all the while. Eventually he decided that all was well and allowed his head to be rubbed for a moment. But there was only a moment to be spared. In ten minutes Tom had taken out the saddle from the place where he had cached it, and the journey of the day was started. Before he had gone two miles, he looked back to a height and saw them coming, the stream of a score of dogs and fully as many riders.

He climbed into the rougher country, for it was there that Jerry could make progress that defied the imitation of men on horseback. From another eminence he stared down and saw that two other packs were out, two other groups of hard riders were following them.

These things, however, he viewed with only a dim concern. He would break their hearts before the day had ended. But he had more to do than simply avoid a few posses. Far away was the place where Dick Walker had ended his evil life and been buried. Thither he must go and hunt around the place for the trail of the murderer. If he could find that trail, if it would lead him to the man, if he could extract the confession from him, then he was free to ride down into Turnbull and meet Gloria unafraid. But how many *if*s lay between!

All that day he worked swiftly through the mountains. Among the rocks, he descended the steep places on foot, at a run. He climbed the difficult ridges seated on the back of Jerry, and he covered the open stretches on the back of the stallion. Here and there he stopped, in favorable places, to lay out trail problems that occupied him five minutes, but which would take the pursuit ten times that long to unravel. In the twilight he found and shot a deer, which provided amply for himself and Jerry. And it was still the dark before dawn when he started on the trail again. In the mid-afternoon, he found the heap of rocks that marked the grave of Dick Walker.

As for the trail of the true murderer—it was like hunting for a needle in a haystack. In the first place, days had intervened since the murder, and rains had washed down the soil. In the second place, the party of Themis had trampled all the region around the grave.

So, while Peter grazed and Jerry dug for roots, Tom cast a corkscrew trail around the place, cutting for signs with an eager diligence. Darkness closed on him, and still he had not succeeded. With the dawn, he was up again and at it, hunting feverishly now, for the posse must be close upon his heels. In the mid-morning he found the first thing that might be of assistance.

It was the empty shell of a .45-caliber bullet, such as had been fired into the head of Walker. It lay a full mile from the place of the shooting in the direction of the eastern mountains. Of course, it might have been thrown there by anyone. Any member of the Themis party might have gone out this far and taken a shot at a rabbit and then thrown the empty shell out of his gun. But there was a chance in ten that it was the shell belonging to the slug that had killed Walker, and in that case the place where it lay meant something to Tom.

He calculated exactly a line between that spot and the site of Walker's grave. If that line were projected into the mountains, it might give him the course that the slayer had taken. But the projection pointed straight at a mountainside, and certainly it was not probable that a fugitive would take that steep ascent instead of sticking to the cañons where he could have made far better time.

But Tom could not stay to argue probabilities. Possibilities were all that he could work on. He struck ahead, aiming his course with nicety for the very peak of the mountain, riding in just the course that a horseman would have been most likely to take if he had ridden in that direction.

By noon he was halfway up the side of the mountain, but there had not been the ghost of a sign to encourage him along the trail. Here he paused while Jerry busied himself with a chipmunk's burrow. After half an hour's rest he went on again until he reached the mountaintop early in the afternoon.

There he found a small spring welling out of the ground. The sight of it excited Tom. Since dawn, he had covered a stretch of ground that would have made a good day's march for an ordinary horse and man. Even Peter was a little wearied by his efforts. If the murderer had in fact taken that trail, the sight of running water must have been too great a temptation to him. Here he would surely have camped, even if he did not build a fire.

But there was no sign, still. From the pine saplings no tips had been cut to make a bed. If deadwood had been cut, it was impossible for Tom to find the place. Although some of the little, dead shrubs might have been pulled up by the roots, the rains would have washed the holes full of sediment. He looked uneasily at the tumble of stones around the spring, and his stanch heart began to fail him. To be sure, he had learned patience in an incomparable school, but he felt that the trail had vanished into thin air if, indeed, it had ever been a trail at all.

Jerry came lumbering from his root digging and began to tumble the stones over. Under some he found grubs that were licked up by that restless, red tongue. Under others he found nothing. But he went on carelessly until a great, 200-pound boulder was tugged over for the mere sake of showing his strength, perhaps, and he began sniffing at the dark undersurface, all sweating with moisture. His growl drew Tom nearer. He looked down to the bottom of the rock for the want of something better to do. It was very dark, indeed. The moisture alone could barely account for its blackness. All the rest of the boulder was a dull gray. Suddenly he leaned and drew a fingertip across the surface of the stone. The tip was blackened by the contact, and Tom straightened with an exclamation of satisfaction.

There was only one way to account for that thin layer of soot. A fire had been built near the stone, which had later fallen upon its face. It must have been a recent campfire that had done the work, no matter if other traces of the fire were lacking. The heavy winds and the rains might have washed all other symbols of it away. This one was enough to set the heart of Tom on fire with hope.

He went back to the head of the mountain to reconnoiter the hollows and the valleys beneath, and there, to be sure, he saw them. The wind fanned his face gently, and it carried to him a faint echo of the clamoring dogs. There they streamed, small as ants in the distance, and behind them was the little army of the hunters. Tom frowned and shrugged his shoulders. It was not for fear of them, to be sure. But how could he follow and untangle the mysteries of this dim trail while these men followed on his trail? His hand tightened grimly upon the barrel of his rifle, but he restrained himself. After all, that was not what he must do. There were strange movements of repulsion in his heart of hearts at the very thought of firing upon a human being. He turned his back on the scene with a murmur of disgust and headed for Peter.

Once in the saddle, he struck out along the hillside at a fast clip. It would have been difficult going for another horse at a run, but Peter negotiated the rough ground at a round gallop. He had not spent six years following the wild trails where Tom and the grizzly led him without gaining some of the instincts and the powers of foot of a mountain sheep. He knew by the back of the soil where it would slide and where the apparently loose gravel would hold fast. He knew how to weave among the trees without diminishing his pace. He knew how to conserve this strength in the climbs, how to go deftly in a serpentine course down abrupt slopes, and then to whirl in a wild gallop through the valley.

That was what he did now as they cut across the mountain slope, then doubled back over the peak, went down the farther slope, opened up at a terrific speed across the more level going in the lowlands, and climbed again, toward evening, into the rugged cliffs, as though they were heading definitely north after the feint of the day before into the east.

As the early twilight came, still bright on the upper mountains, they reached a swift, shallow, snow-fed stream. Into that icy water he rode Peter, with Jerry grunting behind. Although the grizzly had been distanced across the low country, he had more than made up for the lost ground when it came to climbing in the rough hills. Up the stream they waded for a distance, came out on the same side of the stream on which they had entered, and circled back toward the creek, which they entered close to the first point, then crossed to the farther side, Jerry following behind the stallion, and made another swift semicircle on the farther shore. Around they went again in a larger circle, then followed with weaving in and out, and finally dropped straight into the stream, stumbling over the boulders, passed up a branching runlet hardly large enough for them to walk in, and came out again at the head of the runlet upon some great, flat slabs of granite where no visible print of their trail could be left, and where the thin and wandering current of snow waters would probably wipe out most of the scent for a considerable distance.

Over these rocks they went for some distance and at length struck off again through the broken-ridge country. It might take an hour, it might take a day before the trailers located the solution to that puzzle, although by this time they knew many of his tactics by heart.

He had traveled from the peak of the mountain, where he found the sooty stone, over a long, loosely irregular arc. Now he headed, on the almost level plateau, straight across the short cord of that arc and pressed on remorselessly, in spite of the growls and grumblings of the grizzly, until, in the utter dark, he reached the place where, so he felt, the murderer of Dick Walker must have camped before him. There he ventured on his fire. There, after a time, he took a turn in his blankets and fell soundly asleep.

Chapter Thirty

THE END OF THE TRAIL

There was no sign of sunrise when he wakened suddenly and rose to his feet the next morning. But the iron will had roused him after a scant four hours of rest. It was enough. Where the spring water collected in a deep, black-faced pool a little farther down the mountainside, he took his morning plunge. He came back to his own new-kindled campfire, surrounded by rocks, and started the coffee. Then he tended to his shaving. It was the one habit that he had learned from men, for, when his beard began to grow, he had envied the smooth faces of the men he saw, and finally, spying on a campfire in the early morning, he had seen a man shaving. That same razor and strap and brush and soap were mysteriously stolen from the lucky prospector's kit that night, while he slept. In its place there was left a bundle of four fine fox skins. So it was that Tom learned shaving. He had envied the short hair of men, also, but he could not cut his own unless he hacked it off close to the roots with his knife and left a ragged mass covering his head.

Bathed and shaved and breakfasted, he was still too early to take the trail. But in a few moments the quickly coming mountain dawn began, and he looked about him. All around the place were the trails of men and dogs and horses. The pursuers had rested for a time at this point in the trail, well wearied by the labors of that day, as they might have reason to be. But what would they feel when they discovered that that long loop to the side was merely a detour? Tom smiled as he thought of their faces. His ears rang in imagination with their profound oaths. Then he headed down the mountain slope.

He went on until noon, still carefully maintaining that line that he had cast ahead from the crest of the mountain toward the higher peaks. Another deer fell to his rifle then, with a long-range shot. He paused to cook and eat, and let Jerry feed his full. It was a two-hour halt, but two hours of rest in the middle of the day is an excellent measure on a long trail. When he began again in the middle of the afternoon, it was at a pace as brisk as that of his morning spurt. An hour more, and he came on what seemed to him another proof that he was following the correct trail. It was the indubitable sign of a campfire that had spread into the surrounding brush and almost started a forest fire, save that the camper had beaten it out in the nick of time before it spread to the trees.

No rains could hide the scars of that fire. So on went Tom, confident now that he was running in the right direction. He struck up above timberline, crossed a great range of gleaming stone cliffs, and dropped onto the farther side. Was he still on the line, he wondered, as he camped that evening?

Next day he went on again, and it was in the middle of the morning that he came on the first continuous trail. Well worked in along the moist bank of a stream, he found the print of a horse and a dog, and yonder was still the dent of a man's knee where he had stopped to fill his canteen. Of course, it might not be the man he wanted, but from that point he ran on snatches of the trail repeatedly. As a matter of fact, he had traveled in two days as far as the other had traveled in four, and the trail was freshening every moment. Now Jerry began to take an interest, and Tom welcomed his assistance, for there is no more able trailer than a clever grizzly. Men have worked to follow them for the sake of a photograph for two weeks or a month at a time, and never sighted them. More often than not, they have turned back to dog the hunter's steps. At the end of the trail puzzle he finds that the great brute has spent half the day working trail problems for the man to solve, and the other half has perched himself in a safe look-out to enjoy the labors of his enemy.

So it was that Jerry regarded the tracks of the man, the horse, and the dog, got their faint scent in his sensitive nostrils, and finally forged ahead, showing the way to Tom. It was far surer to follow Jerry's lead, but it was slower. Yet Tom, full of anxiety lest the posses overtake him again, allowed the bear to take his own course, only urging him on now and again.

Another day went over his head, and now the trail was so clear that even an amateur could have deciphered it. The horse was shod on three feet. The fourth was bare, and a chunk was broken out of one side of the overgrown hoofs— the right fore. The man wore boots with high heels, sloping to a rather meager supporting surface like modification of cowboy boots, well nigh. Wherever he got down from the saddle, he left prints that showed that both heels were badly turned over and leaned to the outside.

He was a big man, Tom observed by the length of the stride. He was a heavy man, as he could tell by the depth of the impression. That it was a horse as small as the rider was large, was an equally clear deduction and taken from similar testimony. Moreover, it was an expert shot in whose trail Tom rode. He could tell by scars that he had found on a slender sapling at one side of the trail. The tree had been carefully cut in two with five shots, placed so nicely, side by side and in a perfectly straight line, that each orifice neatly touched the next.

Tom examined the tree with care. The caliber of the bullets was .45. He had done that shooting at thirty yards with a Colt then. Even Tom himself could not have improved upon it. Still more, they must have been quick, casual shots such as a man aims to make, such that hand and eye are in faultless practice.

No sooner did the trail become clear than Tom increased his pace, and the fear of the mellow-tongued voices of the dogs of the posse began to disappear when, on the middle of a sunshiny afternoon, he came on indisputable proofs that the trail that he was following through a pine forest had been made only an hour or so before, at the most. If this were indeed the man who had killed Dick Walker, he must be essentially lazy, for, after the first spurt away from the site of the murder, he had gone ahead with marches so short that a child could have made them on foot from day to day. Tom could have covered four times the average distance and never been hard pressed by the labor. But here were the pine needles recently pressed down and unlifted by any wind since the footprints were made. Surely the goal would not be far off.

At least, he would take no chances. He galloped Peter to one side half a mile or more and left him in a small hollow thickly fenced with trees. There he left him with Jerry, secure in the knowledge that nothing would make them budge until he returned and gave the order for a move. Then he struck off through the woods at a run, with his revolver and cartridge belt only. He cut back to the trail of the man and horse and dog. Along this he continued running for a mile 'until the barking of a dog not 100 yards away caused him to slacken his pace.

He came almost at once to a small clearing among the tall trees where a great dog that was apparently a cross between wolf and hound—heavy as the one and long-legged as the other, a huge, fierce brute—was raging around the bottom of a small sapling in the top of which a tree squirrel was perched, chattering with terror. At one side stood a small pinto with the sweat mark still dark on his back and the saddle thrown down just inside the open door of the log cabin. Over the cañon, smoke was curling from the chimney. But the man of the house was standing by the tree, laughing at the terror of the squirrel and the wild fury of the dog.

At sight of that man, the blood of Tom turned to ice, for it was the man who had died in his cave come to life! There was the same gigantic body. There was the same dense growth of black and curling beard. There was the same pair of keen, wickedly active, little eyes. He stood in riding boots, very much like a cowpuncher's, but slightly wider at the toes. He wore overalls and a flannel shirt that had once been red but that was now faded to a short of grisly pink. It was open at the neck. His outfit was fittingly completed with a rag of what had once been a black felt hat. As to the age of the big man, Tom judged him in spite of the heavy beard to be only in his later thirties—the very prime of his muscular life. But, first and last, he noted the boots, the heels of which had sagged well outward under his gigantic weight.

He was busy now bending the sapling. He did it with one hand, with a suggestion of strength in reserve that appalled Tom. He brought down the top of the sturdy young tree until the great hound, with a bound, almost reached the tree squirrel. The latter would run down the trunk, squealing in terror, only to recoil as it neared the hand of the man. So the dog barked and raged, and the man laughed as though his joy in the torture was almost more than he could endure.

At length, a hard shake dislodged the squirrel with such force that it was flung far through the air, struck the ground hard a short distance from the tree behind which Tom was standing, and then raced for safety in the same tree. The dog, meantime, had darted instantly in pursuit with a whine of joy, and Tom saw that in another instant the great jaws would clamp over that small, terrified morsel of flesh.

He could not resist, although it was a wild, incautious thing to do, as he knew. He leaped from his covert with a shout. The dog veered from him, and the squirrel took advantage of that moment to gain the tree and dart up into its branches. There it ran out on a limb, high enough for safety, and chattered its contempt and disgust in the general direction of the dog. The latter began leaping as high as it could in the air, howling dismally in disappointment. But Tom had no longer any thought for either the squirrel whose life he had saved or the dog. He looked up to the master of the latter and found that he was facing the muzzle of a revolver.

Chapter Thirty-One

A FORMIDABLE FOE

There are some men whose minds grow hazy and dim in the crises. There are some whose mental acuteness is a thousand-fold redoubled. Tom Parks was one of these. He saw every detail of the body of the big man. He saw the very bending of the fore-finger around the trigger. With the same glance, he looked into the mind of the fellow, down to his heart of hearts, and what he saw was relentless brutality—an unending store of it. He saw cool and quick decision, too, and the readiness for action that marks the fighting man, made such by nature and trained to per-fection.

"Just get your hands up over your head, son," the other was saying. "Just get 'em up there," he drawled with mur-derous slowness through his teeth, "and keep 'em there."

If there was hesitation in Tom's mind, it did not outlast the fifth part of a second. Then he drew his hands up and stood with them raised obediently above his head.

"Well," said the big man, "say your prayers."

Tom set his teeth. He was incredulous, and yet there was a wicked devil in the eye of the other that told him that any-thing was possible. He saw the forefinger increase its pres-sure. The gun exploded. But at the last instant the muzzle was twitched up. Something dropped with a light crashing through the branches of the tree behind Tom.

"Well, Tiger, eat 'er up," said the big man calmly, and he

added to Tom, lowering his revolver and dropping it into his holster: "You've got your nerve, stranger. You're steady enough."

"I thought that was the end," said Tom with equal quiet.

"All right," said the other and grinned. "You had something coming to you for robbing Tiger of that squirrel. He had the squirrel coming, and you had something coming, too. Now I guess that we're quits. You can put your hands down if you want, partner."

There was no misunderstanding the attitude of this giant. He was perfectly willing for Tom to go for a gun if the latter so desired. His confidence in his ability to get out his own Colt beforehand was profound. There was even a malignant twinkle in his eye that suggested that he would welcome such a clash.

But Tom was not ready to fight, certainly not ready to kill. In the first place, what he wanted from this man was not his death, but, rather, all that he knew concerning the murder of Dick Walker, and, now that he confronted the fellow, it occurred to Tom for the first time that the extraction of a confession might be an affair of considerable difficulty. He had followed the trail blindly. Now that one half of his work was done, there was another half before him, about the accomplishment of which he had no idea. Besides, the mere physical subduing of the big man seemed an impossible task. Behind him the dog was champing and growling noisily at the body of the poor squirrel. It seemed indicative of the power of him of the black beard. That might not be the only death in the clearing before night came.

"Now that we're friends," said the big man, "who might you be?"

"My name is Tom Parks."

"I'm Bill," said the other. "Glad to know you, Tom."

But he made no attempt to shake hands. The right hand rested on his hip carelessly—and near the butt of his gun.

"How come you by this way?" he continued.

"I was lonely," said Tom.

The other grinned, but made no direct response. "And you come on foot, too?" he said.

"No . . . on a horse," said Tom.

"Where's the horse?"

"I thought I'd leave him a little ways off," answered Tom, "until I'd scouted around a bit."

The big man ceased smiling. "You wasn't just sure what sort of folks I might be, eh?" he said.

"I didn't know you," said Tom as gravely as before. "I thought that I'd take a look and see for myself."

"Till you saw Tiger take a dive for the squirrel . . . then you showed your hand?"

"That was it," said Tom. "I hadn't intended to."

"Well," said Bill, "Tiger has the squirrel." He waited, apparently ready to be taken up on this score, but, since he was not challenged, he went on: "I'm glad to see you, right enough. But if you see anything around these diggings that you take a fancy to, just pay me in coin, will you, and not in fur?"

Tom started, and the other laughed heavily, but not with such abandon that his right hand stirred from its strategic position or his eyes for an instant left off their watch.

"Sure," he said, "I knew you the minute I clamped eyes on you. There ain't so many that go around with long hair and homemade clothes these days. I knew you *pronto*. There ain't another man in the mountains that you could be mistook for. What's up, Tom?"

"I was tired of running away from men," said Tom idly. "I thought I'd like to sit down and talk with a man who was in the same position with me."

"The same position? How come?" exclaimed Bill, instantly suspicious.

Tom smiled. "You don't seem to be very near other houses," he said. "Some people may come near your house, but not very many." He turned and waved to the ragged crests of the mountains that on every side pitched up against the sky. When he faced Bill again, he found that the latter was studying him like a hawk. But he wavered in his decision for only an instant. Then he shrugged his heavy shoulders and grinned.

"All right, kid," he said. "I guess you know." Bill winked, but immediately scowled and added: "Not that they got anything on me, but I'm tired of having them with me. I'm tired of being bothered. Can't show my face inside of a town without having the sheriff come around and get clubby. Why, blast their hearts, they ain't got a thing that they can prove on me. All they got is the hope of proving something. But I ain't anybody's fool!" He laughed again, more heartily than before.

Tom nodded and noted that the other waited for him to pass first and then followed half a step to the rear, keeping his guest always under his eye.

"What about the bear?" Bill said. "I'd like to see the bear. Or is that a lie they been telling about you . . . having a bear that you had tamed?"

"It's true," said Tom.

"Well, I'll be hanged," said Bill. "We'll go take a look at that bear after a while. How about eating now?"

"Good," Tom said, but the walls of his stomach were cleaving together with anxiety. "You eat while I talk. I ate this noon."

"You . . . well, son, ain't it time to eat again?"

Tom eyed him in wonder, and then he remembered. Other man sat down to eat three times a day. One meal in twenty-four hours was privation to them, whereas two was a luxury to him.

"Not till tomorrow," he said. "I can't till then."

Bill shook his head. "You're queer, right enough," he decided. "But I can eat for two any day. Are you taking off your gun? It's a pile more comfortable sitting around."

Tom took the hint and stripped off his gun belt and hung it on a peg in the wall. But Bill, while he busied himself taking his food from the frying pan, where it had been simmering, kept his revolver on the edge of the table nearest to him. It was a wretched imitation of a table—two planks joined together over two sawhorses. But, at that, it was almost the only piece of sawed timber in the cabin. The rest was entirely logs. In a corner was a grimy heap of blankets on the floor. There were a few rusted traps; some shirts and boots thrown in another corner; two rifles, a shotgun, and two revolvers hanging on the wall, apparently all well cared for; some sacks of flour and other provisions, a bit mildewed around the bottoms; two stumps leveled on bottom and top had been rolled into the house as chairs. Altogether, it was the dirtiest and most uncomfortable quarters that Tom had ever seen. The fire, gleaming through the cracks of the stove, was the one cheerful center of interest.

The great hound came stalking in, snarled with twitching lips at Tom's moccasin, and then lay down near the stove and glared at Tom out of fierce, red eyes. Whenever the eyes of Tom fell upon him, his lips twitched again, and a growl formed vaguely in the deeps of his throat.

"The dog don't like you," Bill said as he arranged his coffee and ham and fried bread on the table in tin dishes and sat down in front of it, with the revolver still near his plate.

"He don't like you, and, come to think of it, you can't always blame him. He figures that you tried to cheat him out of that squirrel when he had a good chance to catch the little devil. You can't blame him for that, eh?"

"No," said Tom.

At the sound of his voice, the dog growled heavily.

"Shut up!" thundered Bill, and kicked savagely at the head of the dog. But that brute had apparently learned to dodge with expert adroitness. He moved an inch out of range, shifted his eyes to the face of his master with a whine of abject submission, and again resumed his occupation of glaring at Tom.

His presence greatly complicated matters. Bill alone was a handful and more. He was larger than any man Tom had ever seen. Towering six feet and five inches from the ground, with some 250 pounds of mighty muscle, trained hard by the mountain climbing and the mountain work, he was the very picture of Hercules. The meal that was before him was enough in quantity to have fed Tom heartily for two days. But the giant devoured it in great sections. The cords of his huge wrist were as bulky and broad and hard as the tendon of Achilles in lesser men, well-nigh. When he chewed his food, the muscles swelled out along his jaw and made his beard bristle. In addition, Tom had seen enough to know that he was lightning quick with hand and eye. If it came to a hand-to-hand fight, he would be at a more decided disadvantage in having to confront this terrible foeman in such cramped quarters. Altogether, although he had simply proved the superiority of his own strength over the power of ordinary men, and although he would have been confident even now had there been a chance for him to exercise his agility and his endurance over a broader battlefield, he seriously looked upon those enormous hands and those blunt-tipped fingers. But, in addition to all these disadvantages, there was the dog.

That huge beast, as large among his kind, almost, as his master was among men, had formed a confirmed hatred for the visitor. At the first sign of a quarrel with the master, he would fling himself at Tom with teeth large enough and strong enough to tear the throat out of a man at a single bite. Altogether, it seemed that Tom was confronted with insuperable odds.

Yet action he must have, now or never. Somewhere back in the forest, where the yellow light of the late afternoon was sifting through the trees, the posse was coming apace to overtake him. Once they were there, they would not wait to listen to his accusations. Nine chances out of ten, they would simply shoot him on the spot, or else string him up to a nearby tree. Before they arrived, he must have proof to show to the world that Bill was the murderer—or, indeed, was he?

If he were not, it was a lost trail, and with that lost trail was lost all hope of seeing Gloria again. Poor Tom passed the back of his hand across his furrowed forehead.

Chapter Thirty-Two

THE FIGHT

"I've heard tell something about the way you made a fool out of the gang that tenderfoot took up into the hills," Bill was saying. "I've heard tell about it. But you ain't the only one that they've tried to hunt down and ain't been able to. No, kid, you ain't the only one. I had a brother once. They started after him, a good hundred of 'em, but they never got him."

"How long did your brother keep them away?" asked Tom with sudden interest.

"How long?" said Bill. "Why, they didn't never catch him. Eight, nine years ago, along in the spring, he come up into the hills with about a million of 'em after him. But they never put a hand on him. He got clean of 'em all." He laughed and beat his hand on the table until the tins jumped and rattled.

"I sure wish that I'd been around to see how the old boy managed it. He was a hard one, he was. And he just stepped out and walked away from the whole crew of 'em!"

"Eight, nine years," Tom repeated, his idea growing more certain, although he still wanted the proof more complete. "And he's been away all this time?"

"He faded out so complete," said Bill, "that nobody ever seen him again, not even me. But I figure that I know where he went. He had some pals in Australia. That's a good country for a gent that wants freedom. That's where he must've gone."

Tom drew a deep breath. For all the years that lay between, he felt again the heavy hand of the giant in his cave, and heard the deep, growling voice. And Bill was like a larger reincarnation.

"When I got tired having them fool with me," said Bill, "I remembered what he done. I came the same direction, and I done the same thing."

But here Tom shook his head. "Not quite the same," he said.

The joy was stricken from the face of Bill. "Eh?" he grunted, and, staring at Tom, his brute face worked with astonishment and the beginnings of fear.

"I went down to Turnbull," said Tom, "and, while I was there, I heard men talking about you."

"The devil you did!" thundered Bill, and instinctively his huge hand gripped the butt of the revolver, and his glance roved through the door and across the clearing. "Nobody's ever seen me," he continued fiercely. "Nobody but you!" He centered a malignant gaze upon Tom.

"I heard them talking about the killing of Dick Walker," said Tom. "Someone must have seen you in the hills, because they talked about a man of your size. I don't suppose that there is another like you in the mountains around here."

"Nor around no place," Bill said proudly. "Gents of my size don't come along in pairs. But what did they say?"

"They said that not many men were capable of beating Dick Walker. That was why they thought it must have been you."

"It must have been somebody that knew me back in Elkhorn," said Bill thoughtfully. "I had a falling out with Walker there just before I had to leave town. But I left word for Dick that I'd get the skunk sooner or later. I seen 'em make that camp and pile up the stuff after you'd made a fool of 'em and snaked their hosses away. So I went down and called on Walker. They said that nobody could stand up to Walker in a square and fair fight. But I done just that! It wasn't no murder. It was a fair killing. I beat him to the draw. That was all there was to it." He spread out his great arms and grinned with a ghastly triumph. "It was close, at that," said Bill meditatively. "I heard his slug whisper by my ear while he was a-falling. He was dead when he pulled the trigger, but he shot straight enough, at that. Yep, Dick was a hard kid." He nodded and chuckled. It was a horrible thing to Tom to see his exultation. "But they're coming, hunting me?" Bill said suddenly. "D'you hear 'em say that?"

"No," said Tom.

"But what started you on my trail?"

"I thought I'd find you. I found the shell you snapped out of the gun about a mile from the place. That gave me the line you'd traveled. I hit your fire on top of the mountain. . . ."

"You lie!" cried the giant. "It must have been washed away by the rains!"

"One side of a stone was black with the soot of your fire," said Tom.

The other grunted, and his little eyes opened with wonder. "You sure read a trail close," he said.

"Then I came on," said Tom. "After a while, I came on your sign. You were taking your time, you know."

"I can hurry when I want to," said Bill. "I can break their hearts easy enough if they press me. But I didn't figure that I had any call to hurry right then. Otherwise, you wouldn't never have found me, son."

"I suppose not," said Tom.

"But where one gent can follow, another can follow. And by coming over the same way, it'll be like a paved road for the rest of 'em," groaned Bill. "I wish you'd minded your own

211

business and kept away. Why'd you want to horn in and spoil my game? Did I ask you to come down here and call on me like a fool?"

Wild with anger, he fingered the butt of his revolver, and the sweat came cold on the forehead of Tom, yet he managed to meet the glare of Bill squarely.

"I'm sorry," he said. "Shall I put some wood in the stove?"

"Go do it!" snapped Bill.

Tom rose leisurely, stretched, looked out of the doorway into the sunlit clearing, and listened again. Far, far away, like a ghost on the steady wind, he had heard the baying of a pack of dogs. Why did not Bill hear it? But when he turned, he saw that the face of the larger man was not intent in listening. Perhaps his ears were less keenly attuned. At any rate, it meant that the time of Tom was short.

He turned to the stove, took off the lids, and then leaned to pick up a chunk of wood. He reached for the largest and heaviest stick, and, as his fingers closed around it, something like the passing of a shadow, a chill sweeping over his spine, made him wince away just as the hand and the heavy, clubbed revolver of Bill shot down past his head.

Full of suspicion of this unbidden guest, Bill had not been able to get rid of him with a bullet so long as he was unarmed, but the moment his back was turned the conscience of Bill was at ease. Only that lightning dodge to the side had saved Tom from a crushed skull.

He whirled like a cat and struck at the flash of the gun. The billet of wood hit the hand—the gun was knocked spinning toward the door and through it. The roar of Bill, as he jerked back his wounded hand, was as loud as the roar of Jerry in a moment of fury. Tom sprung back, appalled—and received the teeth of Tiger as the big brute fastened his grip on Tom's leg. Yet he dared venture hardly a glance at the dog. One look, and he struck with all his force. The heavy stick landed squarely across the eyes of Tiger and dropped him with a groan, but the blow snapped the stick across and left Tom unarmed to meet the rush of the giant.

All the advantage of his agility was gone. In an instant the giant had closed on him. He could only duck his head under a blow that would have knocked him senseless, never to reawaken. Then the huge arms were wrapped around him. But, in ducking with lowered head, he had thrown his left elbow before him. The enveloping pressure of the big man drove that elbow like a spear into the bones of his chest.

The pain made Bill shout, and in that instant Tom whirled out of the grip of the giant. But so tremendous was the strength of Bill that the tattered remnants of Tom's buckskin shirt remained in his hands, and Tom was naked to the waist. Bill snatched a rifle from the wall—no time to level and aim it—and he flung it at Tom's head. It flew past him as he swerved. Instead of running, as the giant had expected, Tom darted in and flashed both hands into the giant's face.

Trained by many a bruising combat with Jerry to strike speedily beyond conception and with pile-driver force, Tom raised a red welt on the cheek of Bill with one of those blows, and the other slashed the flesh over a cheek bone and let the blood flow in a stream down his face.

Bill struck in turn with all his might. But he had been stung, and hurt men strike short. Just past the face of Tom his blow swept, and the long, darting arms of the smaller man rammed home again into the face of Bill. In either hand there was force enough to have dropped a common man, stunned and helpless, but the solid jaw of Bill took the blows and telegraphed only a faint shock and a small pain to that small, brute brain.

But he was blind with utter rage. He came in, head down,

to crush Tom against the wall. It was like trying to corner a wildcat. He struck thin air and battered himself against the logs. Before he could turn, he received a blow like that of a four-pound sledge swung by a strong hand, landing just beneath and behind his ear. This time he was staggering. He reeled around and met a volley of cutting blows that brought a fresh trickle from his nose and cut his mouth. But here, again, strokes that would have stunned a prize fighter were merely like the sting of a spur to Bill. His slow brain quickened into life again. He saw clearly, and knew that he could never stand at a distance and exchange blows with this shadowy enemy who seemed to carry a hammerhead in either fist. He lowered his head and came in again, but more slowly, his arms outstretched to grip his enemy.

Chapter Thirty-Three

WITH THE POSSE CLOSE BY

For every foot the giant advanced, a pair of driving blows crashed against his head, and just as he thought he was sure to close and set his crushing hands on Tom, the latter flung himself to the side. One hand gripped his shoulder. He tore himself out of the hold, even though those terrible fingers flayed off his skin as though they were iron pincers. A crimson trickle ran down his body as he whirled and struck again.

Bill swept a roundabout swing at the head of Tom. It was like striking at a bobbing cork. The blow went wild, and his ribs sagged an instant later as both fists whipped home into his body. This was far other than blows to the head. His fat abdomen was not meant to withstand such shocks. A mist of sickness clouded his eyes. With a groan he rushed once more, and once more his arms closed on empty air.

He was despairing when he turned. His face had been cut to ribbons. One eye was almost closed. Blood trickled over the other, and still that terrible phantom swayed and dodged before him, and, when he struck, his arm lunged through nothingness.

If only he could get to close quarters. He plunged in again. And again he saw the smaller man waver in a feint to one side, then plunge to the other, but, as he leaped, his foot landed on the barrel of the fallen rifle, which slipped and rolled under his weight. Down went Tom and sprang up again like a bounding rubber ball. But it was too late. That instant had given Bill time to close, and now with a savage shout of joy he flung himself on Tom. One arm passed around the body of Tom. The other hand fastened on his throat, and he whined and sobbed with hysterical joy.

It seemed to Tom that the tendons of his throat were being sprung asunder from the bone. The blood rushed into his face. His eyes swelled out. In vain he clubbed his fists and beat them into that bleeding face. The giant laughed through his teeth and increased his pressure.

A sound of rushing, tumbling water poured into the ears of Tom. Yet he fought swiftly, even though a veil was falling over his senses. He pressed one arm up between himself and the chest of Bill. He passed that arm over the wrist that was beneath his chin. On that leverage he cast a resistless pressure by leaping off the floor and spinning his whole weight into the air. The grip was torn from his throat.

He pitched to the floor, but the giant had toppled, also, and they regained their feet at the same time and stood swaying and exhausted. In three brief minutes of battle they had poured out all their strength.

Then it was that condition began to tell in favor of Tom. To be sure, Bill was well conditioned himself, but he had never known the life of exposure and hardship that was Tom's average life. His muscles had not been turned into so much seasoned whipcord. The exertions had sapped his wind. But two deep breaths dragged into Tom's straining lungs revived him once more.

He slipped aside from the next rush of the giant, whirled, and met him with a blow behind which was his entire power. His fist landed just beside the point of the big man's chin. The shock of it sent a numb tingle to Tom's shoulder, but it stopped Bill in his tracks.

The left fist followed the right, made doubly strong by an electric spark of hope. He cried out softly with joy as the giant gave back with a groan of despair and bewilderment. He lunged again and suddenly, with the terror and the joy of a gambler taking a last chance. Tom stood his ground, his back to the wall, and struck again with all his might. Again the blow landed on the point of the giant's jaw.

Constant hammering will make the staunchest stone crumble. While the first strokes had hardly fazed Bill, the continual dinting of those iron-hard fists had had an effect. A numb area had been growing in his brain. Now it seemed to Tom that the knees of the big man sagged a little under the weight of the punch. At least, it stopped him short again.

He swung his thick arm, and, taking another chance, Tom allowed it to land. But there was still weight enough in that tired arm to lift him off his feet as the fist struck his chest and sent him crashing into the wall. With a gasp he rebounded, braced himself, and drove both fists again into the face of Bill. And again he stopped the big man.

He discovered that there was a world of difference between hitting while on the run and striking while both his feet were planted. He saw the head of the giant roll, and crimson spattered out of the clogged wet beard as he struck. He shifted in a little, and again, with feet spread and planted, he struck. The jaw of Bill drooped. His eyes grew blank. Vaguely he swung at the head of Tom, and the latter stepped in and shot his own fist inside the arc of that swaying arm. The blow landed fair and true on the jaw. That jaw was loose now. Tom felt it give horribly, as though the bones were broken, and Bill slumped to his knees, his back against the wall. It was a grim thing to do, but there could be no chances taken with this brute of a man. Tom crouched and struck again mercilessly. The blow drove the loose head back against the logs. And Bill toppled forward on his face and lay, immense and sprawling, on the floor.

As Tom stood above him, weak-kneed all at once, and gasping for breath, hardly able to realize that of his own power he had been able to beat the giant to insensibility, something which had been forming in his brain as a vague worry now grew clear and defined. It was the baying of a dog pack growing momentarily closer. The posse was near at hand.

He ran to the door and closed and bolted it. He went back to the fallen body that was now groaning. With a cord he secured the wrists and then the feet of the big man. Last, he turned the giant upon his back, then tugged the inert figure to a sitting position, back against the wall.

Bill opened his eyes and looked wildly about him. He glared at Tom with a slow comprehension of what had happened. His jaw sagged as though another blow had landed in the clotted beard at the point of his chin.

"Well," he said finally, "that was a pretty good bout." He tried to laugh. The result was a horrible mimicry of mirth. It ended as he saw the grim face of Tom and the naked torso striped with crimson that had flowed from Tom's torn throat.

"Stand up," said Tom.

The giant rose obediently, swaying on his bound feet.

First Tom reërected the fallen table. "Now sit down there," he said, pointing to a stool that he had placed near the table.

Bill hopped clumsily on his bound feet to the stool and sat down. Tiger, beginning to waken from his swoon, groaned feebly. That sound was echoed by an ear-filling burst of music from the approaching pack, and Bill gasped with terror.

"What's that?" he cried.

"The posse," Tom answered. "They're coming to get me for the killing of Dick Walker. But they'll get you, instead. Bill, you're going to write on the top of the table . . . 'I killed Dick Walker.' And after that you'll put your name under it. Do you hear?"

The tongue of Bill lolled out across his lips. He stared, fascinated, at Tom.

"D'you want me to put the rope around my neck?" he gasped.

"If I hadn't dodged you a little while ago," Tom said quietly, "they would have run you down for murder. It's all one, Bill. Write on that table. Here's some charcoal that will do." As he spoke, he passed a rope around Bill's waist, fastened his left hand to it, and loosened the right. He picked his own revolver out of the holster hanging on the wall. He leveled it at the big man.

"Write!" he commanded.

But Bill, shuddering, shook his head. The baying of the pack came crashing through the forest. There was hardly a minute left to Tom. Another thought came to him. The poker when he opened the stove had been allowed to tip into the fire. He lifted it out. The end was red-hot. He knew that Jerry dreaded fire with a consummate fear. Might not this huge beast of a man have the same fear?

He leveled the white, gleaming end of the poker close to the forehead of Bill. "Write," he commanded, "or I'll write with this in your face!"

"No, no," groaned Bill. "Lord! Get that thing away. I'll write!" With sagging jaw, whining like a beaten dog, he scratched the words across the surface of the table:

I killed Dick Walker.
Bill McKenzie

Chapter Thirty-Four

THE SHERIFF TAKES TWO

Lest he should erase those precious words with a sweep of his hand, Tom fastened both hands behind Bill again. Then he stepped to the door of the cabin, threw it open, and stood outside, near the wall of the little house, just as the tumult of dogs poured out from among the trees and streamed across the clearing toward him. Behind him, he heard the voices of men and the crashing of their horses among the trees.

As for the dog pack, it recoiled from this human quarry and stood about him in a loose semicircle, snarling and howling to show that the enemy was at bay. A moment more, and the hunters themselves came.

They came in a straggling body, a full score of them, and others, distanced by the hard going, were still busily working through the more distant woods. What Tom saw first was the face of Hank Jeffries, with Si Bartlett riding at his side. At sight of Tom at bay, Jeffries jerked out a gun. But Bartlett knocked down his hand.

"Steady up, Hank!" cried Bartlett. "He's surrendered. He'd rather get his neck stretched than be salted away with lead. Sheriff, this is your lucky day."

This to the sheriff, as the latter burst out of the forest on a sweating horse. When he saw what prize had been reserved for him, he threw up his hat with a wild shout. After that, he flung himself out of the saddle and came forward, gun in hand—came slowly, as one who approaches a dangerous and treacherous quarry. But Tom stood without moving, leaning his naked shoulders against the wall of the cabin. The wind was blowing his long hair aside. The blood was drying on his chest, over which his long, brown arms were folded. It was no wonder that the sheriff came slowly.

Sheriff Cassell halted and kicked a dog out of his way. The pack stopped its yelling. In the background, the swarm of horsemen stopped their shouting in wonder at what they saw.

"Are you the man called Tom Parks?" asked the sheriff, conscious of the many eyes that rested on him, conscious, too, that this day he had made a name for himself among the most famous of manhunters, and that the job of sheriff was his for life if he wanted it.

"I am Tom Parks," said a deep, quiet voice.

The little sheriff took a step nearer. "I arrest you," he said, "in the name of the law. From this moment whatever you say may be used against you in court. Hold out your hands."

They were obediently offered. Over the strong wrists the steel of the handcuffs was snapped. Every man in the posse breathed more freely now that those sinewy hands were helpless.

"Why am I arrested?" Tom asked.

"For horse stealing," the sheriff said slowly, "for burglary, for grand larceny, and for petty larceny, and for the murder of Dick Walker."

"For horse stealing first!" cried Hank Jeffries, who had thrown himself from his horse and stepped to the front, his lean face contorted with rage and satisfaction. "And that's enough to hang you." Then he struck Tom heavily in the face with his fist.

The big man did not stir—only a small trickle of crimson went down his face from his mouth.

The sheriff turned, raging, upon Hank Jeffries. "Jeffries," he said, "get back in the crowd if you want to keep a whole skin. If Tom Parks had had his hands free, you'd rather've hit a mountain lion than hit him. If you or any other gent lays a hand on him again, I'll start talking with my gun. Get back and keep out of my sight."

There was a deep-throated murmur of approbation from the posse. They had pressed closer, those thin-faced cowpunchers, staring hungrily at the man who had baffled them so long on the trail, hardly able to understand how they could finally have run him down.

"Who's inside that cabin?" asked the sheriff of Tom. "And what hell-fire have you been raising now?"

"See for yourself," said Tom.

The sheriff stepped cautiously into the open door of the cabin and stood there rooted to the floor with a shout of astonishment.

"Bill McKenzie!" he cried. "Boys, we've landed the two prize birds at one throw of the stone. Bill McKenzie!"

There was a rush for the door of the cabin. Then came another shout as the sheriff read off the confession. "He killed Dick Walker!"

Another voice was lifted, a huge voice of half-whining protest. "He forced me to write that, Sheriff. I swear I didn't have nothing to do with Walker's death. He got out a red-hot poker and said he'd jab it into my face unless I wrote that lie on the table and put my name to it."

"Walker is only one you'll answer for," said the sheriff sternly. "There's the killing of old man Wetherby you'll have to answer for, Bill. They've got the proofs of that. Come out here and face Parks, and we'll hear your story, both of you. Two in one day. And two like these. My luck has sure come in a lump. Sam, you've got a pair of bracelets. Clamp 'em on him. That's right. Now cut those ropes away from his feet. Walk out, McKenzie. There's been a man-size fight in here."

The crowd poured into the open. Huge McKenzie confronted his conqueror with the crimson clots still on his beard.

"Tell your story, Bill," said the sheriff.

"I was sitting in there peaceful . . . ," began McKenzie.

"You lie," snarled a voice in the crowd. "There never was a minute in your rotten life when you were peaceful."

"Shut up, Harry," said the sheriff mildly. "Shut up and let him talk. Go on, Bill."

"There ain't no use talking here," said Bill. "They ain't aiming to believe me."

"I'll keep 'em quiet till you're through," said the sheriff, "no matter what they believe. Go on, Bill. Tell it to the face of Parks."

"I was sitting in there all peaceful and quiet," Bill began again, "when this skunk came and threw a rope over me. I didn't have no chance. Then he told me he was going to make me write on the table that I'd killed Walker. He told me that he'd done that killing himself, and that you was after him and was sure to get him. I told him that I'd see him hanged before I wrote that lie down. He started in to beat me up. You see what he done to me? Finally he got tired swinging his fists, and started with a stick of wood. But I wouldn't give up till he knocked me out. When I come to, he tried a different gag. He got the poker red hot and said he'd jab it into my eyes unless I done what he wanted me to do. And that's what happened. I had to write, Sheriff, that's the truth and no mistake. I never done nothing about the killing of Dick Walker."

There was a deep growl of anger from the crowd. They turned savage faces of hatred upon Tom. Fair play is the first thing that a Westerner demands.

"Well, Parks," said the sheriff, "it's your turn to talk up and talk up loud, or I can't be holding these boys. Something tells me that they're getting a hankering for hanging you up to a branch. Turn loose and let's hear what you got to say for yourself."

Tom looked quietly round on the circle of malignant faces. But in his heart there was a strange riot of emotions. If these men were infuriated, it was simply because they felt he had unjustly treated another man. If there were such justice in them, it was something surely worth knowing about human nature.

So he began his recital slowly with what Gloria Themis had told him—that there was nothing between him and freedom except the killing of Dick Walker.

"All the rest," said Tom, "she thought could be paid for. I took a man's horse, but I took that horse because he was going to kill Peter. I paid him for that horse afterward. And I've paid for everything else I took. If I haven't paid enough, I'll pay more. I want everyone to see that I'm honest. But when she told me that I could be free if I found the real murderer of Dick Walker, I started out to find him. It was a hard thing to do. Rains had fallen since the killing. But I worked around the place until I found a shell for a revolver a mile away in the brush. . . ."

"A mile away! In brush!" exclaimed someone in the group.

"Shut up!" ordered the intent sheriff, whose honest eyes were fixed on the face of Tom.

"I came on the line from that shell to Walker's grave. I found soot on a stone on top of the next mountain and thought that the killer must have made his campfire there. Then I went on. Jerry . . . that's the bear, you see . . . helped me find the trail. He's very good at that sort of thing."

There was a murmur of interest and wonder from the others.

"Finally I came to this house. I found Bill McKenzie and started talking to him. While we were talking, he admitted he had killed Walker. He told me that, I think, because he understood that I was trying to escape from your posse. But afterward he became suspicious again. When my back was turned, he tried to break my head with the butt of his revolver. I dodged that. His dog caught me by the leg." He turned with a limp and pointed to the crimson-stained rent in the back of his buckskin trousers.

"I knocked down the dog with a stick of wood, and then I fought McKenzie. He nearly choked me to death. You see?" He pointed to the torn throat. "But I broke away. Finally I knocked him down. He could not get up. Then I tied him and heated the poker and made him write that confession. All of this is the truth."

He paused, and a silence of deep wonder fell on the crowd until Hank Jeffries snarled.

"Sheriff," he said, "does it sound reasonable and nacheral that a gent the size of Parks could beat Bill McKenzie? Look at the two of 'em side by side."

Truly it was a comparison that dwarfed Tom.

"There is a way of proving what has happened," said Tom. "Free our hands and let Bill McKenzie fight me again . . . here where the walls of the room don't hem us in . . . where I have room enough to move around. Will you do that, Sheriff?" He was on fire at the thought. The old joy of battle that had thrilled him in the conflict with Bill McKenzie returned.

"I'll do that," said the sheriff slowly. "I'll do that, and, if you can beat him fair and square, it sure will look like you been telling the truth. And if you been telling the truth in one part, the whole yarn will sound pretty much like the real thing. We know that Walker and McKenzie used to be enemies. We know he ain't the first gent that McKenzie has finished."

Here he turned point-blank upon Bill. "McKenzie," he said, "talk out. Here you got a chance to prove that he's a liar. What do you say? Shall we turn the two of you loose and the rest of us stand off and give you room and let you fight it out . . . unless you try to bolt for it?"

Bill McKenzie stared fixedly at Tom, and he saw the whole body of the smaller man quivering with eagerness. A smaller man, to be sure, but one strong enough to have broken a common man to bits. His eye dwelt on the perfect proportions, the thick shoulders, the long and sinewy arms. The conviction came to him that, fighting in the free open, he would be simply cut to pieces as a wolf eats a dog.

His head drooped. "I'll see you dead first," he said. "I ain't going to fight to give you the fun of watching. Damn the whole lot of you!"

Chapter Thirty-Five

TOM'S ENTRY INTO TURNBULL

A premonition of disaster came to John Hampton Themis when he heard the uproar pouring through the street of Turnbull. Why his heart should have fallen so suddenly, he could not tell. But his first thought was one of relief that Gloria was out of town visiting the daughter of a rancher who had taken her to the ranch that morning. Themis put on his hat and ran out to the front of the house in time to see the procession pass through the light of the late evening. Apparently a murmur had run before it and informed the town of Turnbull that something worth seeing was about to enter the street, for the entire population had assembled on front porches and in the street itself.

What they saw, and what Turnbull saw, was, first of all, a stream of lean-ribbed dogs running in tumult. Behind them came half a dozen cowpunchers that had ridden out with the sheriff days before on the trail of Tom Parks. Behind them came the sheriff himself, and at the side of the sheriff was a big man with long hair, dressed in buckskin trousers and a tattered buckskin shirt. He sat the saddle on a magnificent stallion that danced along to the noise of the shouts of the men of Turnbull.

It was Tom Parks. Themis could not fail to recognize at any distance the face of the man who had surprised and attacked him on the bank of the river. It was Tom Parks. But how did it happen that he was returning in the guise, almost, of a conqueror? His hands were free, and he was sitting the saddle on the famous horse he had stolen from Hank Jeffries. There was even a rifle in its case slung under one of his knees, and a revolver was at his hip. Certainly this was not the manner in which a man-killer was brought back to town.

There was another man who better filled the rôle of a prisoner. This was a huge fellow who came behind Parks with his hands imprisoned in steel cuffs before him. He rode on a broad-hipped, powerful chunk of a horse, and all around him were clustered the rest of the posse. His name was flashed up to Themis by a dozen voices: "Bill McKenzie! It's Bill McKenzie!"

But who Bill McKenzie might be remained a mystery to Themis. He waited until the procession had filed past, and then, filled with gloomy apprehension, he trailed in the rear toward the jail, where the procession ended.

Parks and the sheriff and Bill McKenzie and some of the posse had gone inside. But a score of men remained in the street. Around each a cluster of the townsfolk formed and heard the recital of the adventure. Themis joined one of these groups and heard the tale.

It was vigorously told. Nothing was left out of the long and arduous trail that the posse had followed, and how they had been led astray time and again by the deft maneuvers of Tom Parks. Yet they had clung indefatigably to the work, although half a dozen of their number had fallen behind on lamed or exhausted horses. The rest of the party had pushed ahead, hopeless, to be sure, but determined to do their best against this invincible phantom of the mountains.

So, at the last, they had ridden into the clearing and seen the half-naked giant standing beside the wall of the cabin. That scene of the capture was painted with vivid, rough words, and then came the exposé of Bill McKenzie as the real murderer of Dick Walker.

"But when we started on back," said the narrator to his breathless audience, "we kept an eye on Tom Parks all the time. The sheriff wasn't taking no chances, and you couldn't blame him. He had half a dozen of us do nothing but keep around Tom all the time. But before we'd been with him long, we began to see what sort of a gent he was.

"And I'll tell you, boys, that we sort of expected to find him a man-eater. What he turned out to be was white all the way through. No growling or snarling. He talked man and he acted man all the way. Never put up no complaints about the irons. Never done no sulking with his head down. He kept his chin up and looked us in the eye. That's the sort of a gent he is. When a gent spoke to him, he spoke right up and answered back plumb cheerful. He didn't make no secrets out of nothing. Inside a couple of hours we got out the whole story.

"Seems that when he was twelve years old he come across the mountains in a storm with his father and a burro. He got played out walking in the snow and the wind. His father picked him up and carried him down below timberline, and doing that he run himself to death, got pneumonia, and that night, getting delirious, he walked over the edge of the river and was drowned. That kid was left there. He tried to move on down the river, but a lion killed the burro. Then he had to stay there. And he stayed there till he growed up. Only man he seen was a brother of McKenzie that came along and beat the kid up and killed a couple of bears that he'd found and tamed. Tom shot McKenzie and saved the last of the cubs. And that cub is the bear that's been trailing him around ever since. But it sure threw a scare into Parks. He begun to figure that there weren't any good men in the world except that father of his that had died. He figured it was better to live by himself, and he done it. That's the short of his story. But wait till you get a chance to hear him tell it.

"The sheriff believes every word, and he says that no white man in the valley will prosecute a case against Parks for stealing what he always paid for, anyway. I'll tell you one thing . . . no friend of mine is going to prosecute any such case. This Parks is clean all the way through. I don't ask no better man's hand to shake and call friend."

Such was the explosion of the fairy tale of the "wild man of Turnbull valley". The Indian had turned into a white man. The reckless marauder had been revealed as a man who knew nothing of property rights.

"He even got Peter back," said the narrator. "He took Hank Jeffries and the rest of us to the place where he'd left Peter. He'd covered their trail complete. Why, it would've made you open your eyes and blink to see the way that hoss acted. The rest of us scared him stiff. He run for Tom and crowded up ag'in' him like he was asking Tom for help.

"We all looked to Hank Jeffries to see what he'd do. Hank seen it was up to him to act sort of generous. He told Tom that he'd try to ride Peter, and, if he couldn't manage it, he'd give the hoss to Tom free and easy. And that's what he done. He climbed onto the saddle on old Peter, and he started to ride him. Didn't look like there was going to be nothing to it. Peter was scared, right enough, but he answered the bridle like he was thinking the same thoughts with his rider. Tom begun to look sick. But pretty soon Hank made a wrong step. He got so plumb confident that the hoss was broke for him that he touched Peter up with the spurs. It was sure a fool move. Peter seemed to take that as orders for doing a cake-walk up the sky and kicking out a star or two. He raised Cain in seven languages, and inside of thirty seconds he pitched Hank on his head and come running over to Tom, like a dog, and shoved his head down against Tom's chest.

"Well, Hank got up, staggering and raging. He wanted that hoss quick, so's he could blow its fool head off, because he said it was a nacheral born man-killer. But there stood the hoss asking Tom for help, you might say. And there was Tom talking to Peter like Peter was a man. It was sure something to remember, that picture. Then the sheriff he ups and tells Hank that his hand has all been played out, and that he ain't got a trick left for taking Peter. He'd give Peter to Tom by not being able to ride him, and the whole gang of us was there as witnesses to the bargain.

"There wasn't nothing for Hank to do but buckle under, no matter how he hated it, so Tom rode back right on his own hoss, and it was sure a circus to watch them two together. About the end of the second day the sheriff talked things over with us, and then he took a chance. He got hold of Tom and said if Tom would give his word not to try to escape, he'd let him ride with his hands free and do what he liked. After Tom agreed, I'll tell a man that we sure lived on the fat of the land. If we wanted fish, he'd sneak off and drop a hook into a pond, and it looked like the fish came running to get caught. If we hankered after venison, Tom would snoop off through the hills and come back in no time with a deer. It wasn't no starvation party that we rode on, I'll tell a man."

There was more talk like this, but John Hampton Themis had heard enough to confirm his suspicion. When Gloria came back to the town, she would find the praises of the wild man on the lips of everyone. Not only would he no longer be dreaded, but every pretty girl in the town would have a wildly beating heart at the mere thought of meeting this handsome giant who even the men were praising. In that romantic atmosphere, how could Gloria be expected to keep her head about her?

Themis went on into the jail and found it all buzzing with

excitement. The happy sheriff came up to shake hands with him.

"Well, Mister Themis," he said, "if the luck had been with you, your party might have done just what mine did. I give you credit for stirring up the valley for the hunt, at any rate. We profited by the lessons that you taught us. When you come right down to it, he never could have been caught if he hadn't wanted us to take him."

Themis brushed the praise away. "He gets off scotfree, then?" he said.

The sheriff shook his head with a frown. "I thought he would," he said. "But that fellow whose dogs were killed by Parks insists on getting damages. He's worked up a bill for a thousand dollars, nearly. Everybody else has agreed to withdraw their charges. But that gent won't budge. If it wasn't for him, Tom would walk free out of jail. But where can a boy like him find a thousand dollars?"

The mind of Themis was never slow. Now it worked like lightning, reaching far ahead to the future.

"Suppose I sit down and write a check . . . I have my checkbook with me . . . do you think that would set Tom free?"

"Of course," said the sheriff. "We know you, Mister Themis. Your check is the same as gold. But would you do a fine thing like that?"

It was done in half a minute. The check was scrawled, torn from the book, and placed in the astonished sheriff's hands.

"Now," said Themis, "can you so arrange it that I may talk with Parks? Talk with him alone, I mean."

Chapter Thirty-Six

FOR THE HAPPINESS OF GLORIA

It was no easy thing to manage, but eventually the crowd was cleared from the sheriff's office, and Tom was brought in. He stood, tall and silent, in one corner, his quiet, keen eyes fixed upon the face of the millionaire.

"Tom," said the sheriff, laying his hand affectionately on the shoulder of his prisoner, "I'm mighty glad to tell you that we've brought you into town just to turn you loose and set you free again. I was afraid for a while that it wouldn't come out just that way. But Mister Themis, here . . . I guess you've met before"—here the sheriff grinned, but Tom's face retained its gravity—"Mister Themis, as I was saying, has made out a check for a thousand dollars to pay off the only gent that's going to press a charge against you. Well, Tom, I guess you don't know much about what money means. But after you've worked for some of it you will. You'll see that a thousand iron men come slow when a gent tries to save 'em. It's a pretty fine thing that Mister Themis has done. I'm going to leave you in here to talk with him because he wants you to. Afterward, you can walk out of this jail just when you please. If you got no better place to go tonight, I got a bed at my house that ain't working, and I'd sure be honored if you come and put up with us. My wife would make you plumb to home."

It was quite a speech for the sheriff. Moreover, it was a

233

speech that obviously came from the heart. Themis watched with a keen curiosity to see what Tom would say.

"You are a kind man," he said to the sheriff, "but tonight Jerry is wandering back in the hills. He is waiting for me. Peter and I must go to find him. But when I come up to Turnbull again, I shall come to you first . . . to thank you again."

It was neatly turned, Themis felt. The sheriff flushed with pleasure and good will and went, whistling, through the door. As soon as it was closed behind him, the man of the mountains faced Themis again. The latter noted that no word of thanks had passed his lips.

The explanation came at once.

"You have paid me a thousand dollars," said Tom Parks. "What am I to pay you, Mister Themis?"

The latter started. He had not expected this quiet thrust. Plainly the big man was nobody's fool. And Themis flushed a little.

"You are exactly right," he said. "Parks, I shall expect a return."

"I shall make it if I can," said Tom. "What is it that you wish?"

"To keep you from my daughter," said Themis, with a sudden feeling that he must be nothing but utterly honest while he faced those shrewd, sharp eyes, so trained to the following of obscure trails on the mountain and equally keen, perhaps, to look into the minds of men. "What I wish, Tom, is to keep you from my daughter."

Tom Parks paused, and Themis saw that the big fellow was carefully restraining himself and waiting until his emotion should pass over.

Then he said as quietly as ever: "If you were to offer me money for Peter, I should laugh at you. If you were to offer me money for Jerry, I should laugh again. But when you offer me money to keep away from Gloria, to sit where she is sitting, to watch her, to see her and know that she is beautiful . . . if you offer me money in place of that, I cannot even laugh, Mister Themis."

"Tom Parks," said the rich man, more and more amazed by the talk of the big man, "where did you gain an education? What books have you read?"

"Only two," said Tom Parks.

"And what were they?"

"The Bible and the *Morte d'Arthur*."

"That's enough," said the other. "I can't tell you what a difference it makes to me to learn that you know those two books. But I shall go on developing my idea to you. You see that I am at least frank, Tom."

The other nodded.

"Before you can understand me fully, or I you, we must come to an agreement. We agree, in short, that what we are both interested in is the greatest happiness for Gloria?"

"Yes."

"Then let us slip out the rear of the jail where the crowd can't see us and follow you. I want to take you to the house where we are staying."

It was done. They went through the rear of the jail. Behind the houses they circled back through the dark of the night and entered the house that Themis had rented. There they went directly to the room of Gloria. In that room Themis opened a closet door. The shadowy recess was filled with the glimmer of silks.

"If you stay in this part of the country," said Themis, "do you know what you will make each month as a cowpuncher . . . I mean, what you will make in money?"

Tom Parks shook his head.

"Forty dollars," said Themis. "And if you save it all, it makes six hundred dollars a year. Now look at these clothes. There's hardly a dress here that cost less than fifty. Most of them cost more. Yet this is the simplest part of Gloria's wardrobe. She brought this along to rough it in the mountains, as she expressed it. And here are the shoes, Tom. You see this whole rack of 'em?"

Tom Parks took out a dainty slipper. It was lost in the brown expanse of his palm, and he wondered with a faint exclamation at the delicate workmanship.

"And here are hats," said the father, pointing to a shelf piled with them. "After all," he continued, as he opened a great wardrobe trunk filled with other articles of wearing apparel, "this, as I said before, is only a small section of Gloria's clothes. And I wish you to remember, Tom, that a woman's husband is expected to provide for her. Can you give her these things?"

Tom had grown pale. Then he answered slowly: "When a man's stomach is full," he said, "and there is no work to do, the mountains are most beautiful. But even when his belly is flat and he is following a long trail, they are still beautiful."

Themis wrinkled his brows—then nodded. "I understand you," he said. "She has been happy in one way when she had all these things. She will be happy in quite another way if she marries you. I shall admit even more. Gloria is not a girl who needs the finest silks. She could get on with much less. But there is a minimum of that to which a woman is accustomed, which she must have in order for her happiness to be possible. But even that minimum, I'm afraid, you cannot give her. Mind you, Tom, I am showing you these clothes simply to indicate other things. Clothes are a small part of a modern woman's environment. But every other thing that costs money is dear to Gloria. She has never had to consider cost.

She has formed a thousand tastes. Consider only music and the theater. They are not small things in her eyes. There are her friends, Tom, just as dear to her as your Peter and Jerry are to you. If she came out here with you, she would lose all this. And remember again that we are both considering one thing first before all else . . . what will make for the greatest happiness of Gloria?"

The head of Tom lowered. He passed a hand across his forehead.

Themis saw that his face was corrugated with misery. "Now," he went on smoothly, "suppose we pass to my proposal in full. You see that I oppose you now. I wish to keep you from Gloria. She is an emotional girl, full of enthusiasm, easily swept off her feet. If you come near her now, it will be like bringing fire near dried stubble. You see that I am telling you even more than you knew about her. I oppose you now because I cannot tell you what you will be after you've mixed with men and tried to make a place for yourself. Mind you, I don't demand that you make a fortune. All I ask is that you become capable of making a moderately good living. That will be enough. In fact, I have no right to make any demands. It is only that I advance any proposals for the welfare of Gloria."

"Go on," said Tom in a husky voice. "Finish what you have to say."

"Very well. My suggestion is that you go to the East just as Gloria has come to the West. If you will do that, I shall be willing to furnish you with a letter of introduction to a friend of mine who will make a place for you in his business. In return, I ask that for a solid year you do not speak to Gloria or in any way attempt to communicate with her. I send you to the East. I furnish you with enough money to live decently and pay your railroad fare. You, in return, do your best to fit yourself to make a living. At the end of a year, perhaps Gloria will have changed. Perhaps not. Perhaps you will have found a place for yourself. Perhaps not. At any rate, we would both be taking a chance. Does that sound fair to you?"

"Perhaps," said Tom, with the sweat pouring out on his forehead, "she would have forgotten me."

"Perhaps," Themis said honestly, "she would."

Tom walked across the room, came back to the window, and stared into the black night. "To leave Peter and Jerry . . . ," he said.

"If she stayed here," said Themis, "how much more would she be giving up." His heart beat high with hope. There was sympathy, too, in the glance with which he watched the young fellow struggle with his conscience, for he saw that he was dealing with an honest man and a brave man, who did not flinch from the infliction of pain on himself. Themis himself was honest as the day is long. He did not press his point, but waited.

"And you," said Tom suddenly, facing Themis, "are her father. You have a right on her."

"Only to work for her happiness, Tom, my boy, just as you would if you could."

"To leave them both," said Tom slowly. "It is very hard."

"I can manage another thing for you," Themis announced, full of sympathy. "I can ship the horse East for you. As for Jerry, you will bid him good bye for a year."

"But you will send me the horse?" Tom asked sadly.

"Yes."

"Then . . . I accept."

Themis drew a great breath and collapsed in a chair. He did not know before how great had been the strain under which he labored. He had gained a year! A year in the life of a girl is an eternity. He would sweep her off to Europe. He would give her a whirl through Paris. He would surround her with fine young fellows of her own age, her own position. If the year did not bring about results, he could say that he did not know human nature.

"Take my hand," Themis said, and offered it.

That hand was almost crushed by a tremendous pressure.

"We shall neither of us forget," said Themis. "Go back to Jerry and tell him good bye. Then come to me tomorrow. No, better still, I shall meet you . . . behind the Jeffries place, let us say."

"I shall be there at noon," said Tom. He turned to the door. He did not go on, however. A door banged. Light steps came running down the hall. Tom turned to Themis with a face of agony. "It is her step," he said.

"You have given me your word," Themis said anxiously. He rose from the chair. "Not a syllable to her, Tom, or the compact is broken."

The door of the room was dashed open. Gloria stood before them, flushed, radiant, worthy of her name.

"Dad . . . Tom . . . oh," she cried, "I've heard! It can't be true! It's too wonderfully good to be true! And both of you here. . . ."

She fell suddenly silent, staring into the stony face of Tom Parks. She recoiled as he walked past her without a word, passed through the door, closed it behind him, and disappeared with a soundless step.

Then she turned on Themis. "Dad!" she whispered. "What has happened?"

"My dear," he said, "are you going to ask me to explain the psychology of a wild man?"

She looked helplessly, despairingly at him. "I'll follow!" she cried. "I'll find out!" She ran to the door, paused, turned away. "Not a step," she said. "I'll not follow him a step." But she dropped into a chair and sat with clasped hands, watching the face of Themis for an explanation.

But Themis was looking past her and into the future. He was wondering, after all, if he had been right. He carried at least one certainty: Tom Parks was a fighter. He had battled all his life. The winning of Gloria might prove only one battle more that he would win, although perhaps the greatest battle of all.

He looked sadly at the girl's face. Great tears were running slowly down her cheeks. And Themis resigned himself to destiny.